To Pat and the boys

You can tell if a man is clever by his answers. You can tell whether a man is wise by his questions.

Naguib Mahfouz

PROLOGUE

If you and I were to return to Clamford in the Vale, we would find that nothing much has changed in the two years since that infamous statue of the naked Harriet Wilberforce was erected by the bridge crossing.

You might have imagined that her niece and ward, Camilla, had grown bored with the regular pace of life in Brompton Hall, and returned to London, yet she remains.

Millers shop still opens at six in the morning when Cissie and Joan lower the green and white striped awning. The newspaper lad always appears with his ancient bike. The old clock still chimes every fifteen minutes on the dark landing of the vicarage where the Reverend Geoffrey Roper and his clever wife, Julia, continue to fret over their adopted children. Peggy Sudron can be seen most afternoons, pushing Jim around in his wheelchair.

None of the residents have moved away since the astonishing revival of their beloved village was assured by Harriet's generous legacy. None, except for Miss Marcia Bennett, who vacated her little cottage for a Care Home, close to Larchester.

If we spent an hour in the Fox and Grape, we would soon catch up with the gossip, interpreted with unnerving accuracy by the ubiquitous landlady, Sandra Hewitt. Then, we may well be tempted to linger over a couple of drinks to discover more of the strange events that occurred over the previous couple of months.

PART ONE

THE ARRIVAL

CHAPTER ONE

The bronze statue of Harriet Wilberforce shone proudly in the Spring sunshine, untarnished by graffiti. Not a mark or blemish on her. Two harsh winters had not dulled her gleaming smile, nor the intensity of her sculpted eyes, forever fixed on her beloved Clamford in the Vale, her naked defiance catching flashes of bright light from the tumbling river below.

She continued to attract new admirers to this northern outpost. Some folk journey hundreds of miles from unfamiliar parts, even as far as Australia and Japan, to take their selfies next to her. True, there may be fewer visitors now than last year, but no matter, the old girl was still pulling them in.

Ted Smailes floated somewhere in the sunshine. A thin smile tried its best to form on his whiskered face as he attempted to convince himself, once more, of his good fortune. The familiar hip flask had to be discarded last year on health grounds but, at least, he could see his feet once again when standing upright. He couldn't quite remember why or how he got here, watching over the statue, even if his wife, Doris, could. These days, Ted was a different man, everyone said so. The sharpness in those twinkly eyes was a little dimmer these days, and there was less of an edge to his voice. He was seen less often in the Fox and Grape and, after last year's heart attack, Doris laid the law down, insisting he must shed some timber from his waistline. Their boys, Phil and Stuart, did most of the heavy work around the farm, their father's watchful eyes no longer in evidence very much. He must, surely, be a contented chap, he constantly reminded himself, someone who has always known which side his bread was buttered on.

Briefly, for no more than a second, the faces of Jim Sudron and Marcia Bennett shone between a couple of clouds, way up above the trees. He shuddered and gave a little cough.

'Rather them than me.'

April was sliding into May and the day was comfortably warm. It had rained overnight, though only gently. He'd lain awake next to Doris, unable to recall the events of the day that had just passed, but picturing the one that lay before him, it would be a day to walk and relax and get away from the farm.

He leaned back against the plinth on which naked Harriet stood unabashed next to the temporary river bridge crossing she bequeathed to the village as part of her magnificent legacy. Maybe it would always be temporary, for ever fulfilling its promise to provide the vital lifeline between Clamford and the outside world.

'Thank you, Harriet you were a good'un,' he muttered.

Just then, the steady rumble of tyres descended into the valley from the hillside. A large Land Rover sparkled in the sun as it ground to a crunching halt on the gravelly layby next to the bridge; the driver and his passenger, cloth capped, were clearly deep in amiable conversation behind their dark sunglasses.

Ted shuffled to his feet. The driver stepped out into the fresh air, straight backed and confident, leaving his passenger inside the vehicle to talk into his mobile phone. Retrieving his walking staff from the back seat, he tapped the frame of his sunglasses and turned towards the statue where Ted, stationary and vaguely interested now, offered a friendly nod.

'Hello, a fine day, isn't it?'

The gentleman's voice was unusual, resonant and strangely familiar, causing Ted to hesitate before replying. An awkward silence descended while the sunglasses were removed. In that moment, Ted decided that it might be appropriate to offer his hand, which was duly received with a steady grip.

'Your Majesty…this is a surprise.'

King Charles smiled and leaned on his staff to examine the statue more closely.

'Do you live here?'

'Yes, Sir. All my life.'

'Beautiful part of the Country.'

'It is that…'

The King took his time to examine the little plaque at the base of the statue, donated and funded by the Women's Institute, then allowed his eyes to wander, still unshaded, over the naked features of Harriet's bronze figure. A quiet 'tee-hee' escaped his lips as he folded his arms behind his back.

'Toconom.'

'I'm sorry, Sir, I must be going deaf in my old age. I beg your pardon, but I didn't quite hear you properly.'

'Not at all, no, quite alright, just musing. Good to meet you…er?'

'Ted, Sir, Ted Smailes.'

'Well, we must go, Ted. Enjoy your day, won't you?'

Then, with a slight wave, His Majesty turned back to the Land Rover and, inside a minute, was gone.

Ted lay back to resume his position and reflected for a moment on what had just happened. To recount this incident to Doris would be to invite expressions of sympathy and concern from the family, which would not be good, so it would be better to keep it to himself, at least for the time being.

From the hills above, the familiar clicking sound of cycle wheels heralded the swooping of a group of cyclists as they freewheeled down the bank and flew across Harriet's bridge crossing towards the village. One of them blew a kiss to her statue.

Stillness returned, and now only the river and the birdsong could be heard as Ted removed his battered old hat, wiped his brow with a handkerchief and prepared himself for the return journey through the village, back to the farm. Just a few more minutes, that's all he needed. A little more time to stare into the bubbling waters of the river and let the sounds of the Vale, hushed yet full of presence, wrap themselves around him.

A new noise brought his head up.

Just a few yards away.

He was more unnerved than truly startled, but all the same, why hadn't he looked up before now to see the horse approaching?

It was an old piebald, weary and panting heavily. On his back rode a man, whistling and humming a tune unrecognisable to Ted. There was more than a hint of jauntiness about the man's lean body and athleticism, making it tricky to assess his age, he was probably in his forties but could be older. Unshaven, wearing a white tee shirt, faded blue jeans and heavy walking boots, he dismounted to lead the poor beast to the water's edge, whispering close to its tired old head. After a moment or two, he removed a heavy saddle bag from the horse's back and dropped it to the ground.

'A fine day.'

His voice was confident like the King's, and warm but, unlike His Majesty's, ripe with dialect that placed him, Ted reckoned, somewhere from the north, but not local.

Going back home could wait, Ted was in the mood for a conversation.

'It is indeed, have you come far?'

'Aye, you could say that.'

He gave no further clues, as his large hands plunged deep into the saddle bag to remove a small bottle of juice.

As a young lad, Ted found it easy to make pals, loving the thrill of new talk, new games, new mischief. The sensation returned to his body. Instinct urged forward his arm to the stranger who now accepted his strong grip and returned it with a friendly squeeze of the hand and a countenance that revealed clear blue eyes, white teeth and easy smile.

'My name's Ted Smailes, what's yours?'

'Jacob.'

'Pleased to meet you, Jacob, are you just passing through these parts or do you have business in the village?'

'Well, that depends…'

'Sorry, none of my business.'

'No no. That's ok. Just curious to find out what's here, that's all.'

Ted proffered Jacob a knowing wink and glanced up at Harriet's statue, unable to conceal the delight in his voice, 'Well, there she stands in all her glory. I expect like most folk, you've come just to see what the fuss is all about, eh?'

'You could say that.'

The horse paused from drinking the river water and shook his mane to swat away the flies.

Years ago, Ted harboured a dream of owning a racehorse and, without consulting Doris, bought a couple of decent looking mares, but eventually sold them on to a trainer from Larchester. Then there were the Cleveland Bays he used to keep in the stables, the same proud steeds who pulled the carriage for the Waterhouse family wedding. Doris insisted the Bays had to go after Ted's heart attack. Same thing with the hens…selling eggs is too much hassle these days, she said, leave that to Roy Sudron, he's cornered the local market around here. In truth, it was with cows and sheep, that Ted's heart lay, cows especially. Mind you, he reassured himself, if he did buy another horse, it wouldn't be one that looked as knackered a thing as Jacob's old piebald.

'I know what you're thinking, Ted, that poor horse of mine is looking a bit worn these days, but we get around alright. He's good for a few years yet, I reckon.'

'Where do you keep him? Is it far from here?'

'Far enough, I suppose, but we manage. Folk are kind. Farmers and country people like. They give us a bit of feed and somewhere to lay our heads, don't they boy?'

Jacob clicked his tongue against his teeth, and the horse trundled straight to his side.

'What's he called?'

'Joey.'

'Ah, like the War Horse thing…good name.'

'It sort of suits him, I think. Well now, you look like a man of means to me, Ted. You live in Clamford, am I right?'

That was a bit forward. Of course he lived here, where else? Never mind, Ted was really beginning to warm to Jacob, 'Aye. We have a farm on the other side of the village. There's a couple of stables and plenty of feed. You're welcome to keep him there 'till you're ready to move on. What about you, you got somewhere to stay?'

'Who said anything about staying?'

Ted floundered, trying to keep his tone even, 'Sorry, I don't mean to…'

With a reassuring grin, Jacob began to pat his palm against Joey's neck, 'No need to be sorry, I'm only joshing with you. Kind of you to make the offer.'

'Ok. Well, if you need somewhere to stop over, I might be able to help.'

'Yeah? That would be good, I was going to sleep under canvas again but…'

'No need. I own a little cottage just down the lane at the East end. Bought it last year to rent out when the previous owner sold up. It's empty at the moment till the holiday season starts proper.'

'You sure? I don't want to be a trouble, but it would only be for a short while. I can pay my way.'

Aware that he hadn't really thought this through properly, Ted was, nevertheless, warmed up to the idea. A new face to liven things up a bit. A few bob coming in to help things along. Someone different to have a laugh with. They could share a couple of pints in the Fox and Grape. Why not?

The sun was now high in the sky, casting dense shadows and shafts of blazing light through the girders of the road bridge as Joey's hooves thumped their slow rhythm behind Jacob and Ted. It took less than ten minutes to reach the door of Marcia Bennett's old place.

'Here it is. Once we've settled the horse in at the stable, I'll get the keys and we can come back if you like, see what you think, yes?'

'Sounds like a plan.'

'The lady who lived here kept it spotless. I probably paid over the odds to be honest, but she's a sweet old dear and…well…'

'Where is she now?'

'In a care home, she had a nasty fall, left her lame. They fetch her over in one of those little coach things, a transit van, every now and again, to the church or the village hall, whatever. They're very good like that, at the care home.'

'That's good. Look here, Ted, I'd like to give you something up front for your kindness and for my keep and for Joey.'

'No need, honestly. Pay me later.'

'Well, take this for now, call it a bond.'

'You what?'

'Take it, go on.'

He handed Ted a tiny brown envelope, which Ted stuffed in his back pocket without looking at it.

Much later, in the small hours of the night, Ted woke from a soon- forgotten dream and lay on his back, hands on chest, listening to Doris's throaty breathing. Sleep wouldn't return for a while, he could always tell, so he fumbled in the top drawer of the little table next to the bed, where he hid Jacob's envelope. Tomorrow, he'd explain again to Doris about the horse and the cottage arrangement. He will not mention the King. Breathing slowly, he shuffled to the bathroom, fingers wrapped around the envelope. The door clicked shut, he paused, Doris slept on. He pulled at the light cord and screwed up his eyes until they adjusted to the glare before opening the envelope. A single word was written, probably by a strong hand, on a piece of folded paper. The word read: TOCONOM.

CHAPTER TWO

Today, it felt to Ted as if the world had a fresh coat of paint. He had been up and about since six thirty; checking on Joey in the old stable block, then watching over the cow sheds as the milking was completed before settling down to his breakfast.

Doris could barely bring herself to speak to him, 'There's your boiled eggs, if you want to kill yourself with bacon sarnies, you know where the frying pan is.'

'A week at most. I reckon he'll move on after that, you'll see. Anyway, what harm is he doing? Seems a right enough chap to me and he says he'll pay his way, so where's the harm, eh?'

'You haven't a damned clue, have you? You just get an idea in your head and away you go...a complete stranger, we don't know him from Adam. Then there's that mangey old horse. Well, on your head be it. I won't be able to show my face at the W.I.'

She took herself off to the front room and Ted poured himself another cup of tea. This felt like another fine day.

In 'the Lane,' Millers shop had been open, as usual, since six this morning when Cissie lowered the familiar green and white awning. Her sister Joan loaded up the little wooden tables and baskets on the pavement with fresh produce from the gardens of Brompton Hall.

For the last month, the Miller routine had slowed down to where the regulars had noticed tiny but slightly unnerving signs of fatigue.

'Looks set for another lovely day, Joan.'

Cissie waited for the familiar echo of her sister's response, but there was a long pause before she chimed in.

'Lovely day, Ciss.'

There was no doubting now; the ebb and flow, the regular rhythm of their chattering was stuttering. Even so, the routine lived on: the paper boys had been and gone and Roy Sudron had left a good supply of eggs. Soon, they were ready for the morning rush.

Joan clenched her fist against the counter, she seemed distressed, red faced and rooted to the floor.

'Cup of tea, Joan?'

'No Cissie, it's a bit early. This will pass in a moment or two.'

'Have you taken your pills? Shall I call the doctor?'

'Pah! Pills are useless. Absolutely not. I might manage a little walk this afternoon, stretch my legs. Stop bothering, we'll manage.'

'If you're sure.'

'I am.'

A heavy footstep stopped the conversation. A tall man was standing in the shop entrance, a stranger, unremarkable in T-shirt and jeans but for the heavy working boots and compelling smile. His eyes were friendly, his tone warm.

'Ladies, alright if I look around?'

Joan inspected him a little cautiously, her eyes still strained, her hands now rubbing her lower back as she straightened up. Cissie beamed and beckoned him to come in.

'Yes yes. Can we assist? We sell cigarettes, newspapers over there.'

She made a little wave with her arm and quickly glanced at Joan.

'No thanks, don't smoke and never read the papers. Do you have any orange juice, and some bread, butter and cheese?'

'Of course.'

'And some envelopes, please.'

'Yes, we have some plain ones here. Do you need stamps?'

'Plain is fine. No stamps…thanks. Nice store, my name's Jacob.'

In the dim light of the shop, Joan needed a closer inspection. He certainly greeted them both politely enough, she thought, seeing him more clearly now; quite tanned and more than a little weather beaten, taut in body without being too muscular, the hair just beginning to grey around the temples. His eyes were kind, she decided, and the smile genuine, belonging to a man who was certain of his place in the world. She caught her breath and watched him as he moved to the far counter. There was definitely something about this fellow which touched a part of her soul she had almost forgotten ever existed, something that quickened the spirit. An intimate connection that she didn't understand. It was exhilarating. Ralph. Every night she cast a glance at her husband's photograph by the bed, the one she took at Bournemouth a year before he was taken, but she hadn't really imagined his hair, or sensed the warmth from his shirt, not for donkey's years. Until the moment this man walked into their shop.

'You sit down for a minute, Joan, while I serve…Jacob.'

'Yes, alright then, it'll pass in a minute, don't fuss.'

A week ago, she relented and allowed Cissie to place a kitchen chair behind the newspaper counter for such moments as these; she winced, unable to disguise the discomfort and irritation as she slumped down onto it.

It only took a couple of minutes for Jacob to stock up with his groceries and place them in the bag that Cissie kindly thew in as a freebie.

'Sorry about your back pain, Joan, nothing worse than back pain is there?'

Joan's head shot up, unnerved by the over familiarity from a stranger.

'How do you know my name?'

'Sorry…I didn't mean to offend. The other lady said your name…'

Joan's head drooped again, her shoulders sagging.

'No, look, just ignore me, it's very kind of you to show concern, I'm sure, isn't it Cissie?'

'Very kind, Joan.'

He approached the newspaper counter and spoke to the top of her head, 'Have you seen a doctor?'

'Pah! Useless. He's got me on pills, but they're not shifting it. Cissie will tell you.'

'No, that's right, not shifting it, Joan.'

Jacob was leaning in now, 'Can you sit up straight for me?'

Joan looked to Cissie who was staring, blankly, and obeyed.

'Try stretching your arms above your head, as if you're going to wave to someone far away, and say aahh at the same time.'

'Get away with you, you must think I'm daft.'

'Far from it, go on, just for me.'

Joan was smiling now while Cissie chuckled by the cheese display. Slowly, she raised her arms.

'There now, but I will *not* say aahh.'

'Well, say something else then…please, just for me.'

'Like what, hurry up and think of something sensible, my arms are getting tired.'

'Try saying…TOCONOM.'

CHAPTER THREE

There was no give in the old, hard tractor seat when Freddie Bairstow sat on it, alone, drenched in sweat. He could have waited a few days before giving the cricket pitch another cut, but the lads were keen to organise a few training sessions before the match against Larchester. Freddie glanced up again at the clock by the pavilion; he should have been at the abattoir by now, but he'd catch up with work tomorrow. Right now, he had other plans, while there was no one about the place, after a well-earned cup of tea.

The wicket looked flat and straight with no obvious dips or bumps, and that was sure to please Phil and Stuart Smailes in the Fox and Grape tonight. But, for now, there was plenty of time to prepare himself, one more time.

From behind the old wooden pavilion, where he kept the roller and the gang mowers, Freddie rummaged around for the rickety old crate he'd hidden away for the winter, under a tarpaulin. He'd chosen it especially for a specific purpose. It was the perfect size and shape. So far, yesterday and the day before, it had performed brilliantly. Carefully, he placed it at the very edge of the pitch boundary where the ground was not too parched, but particularly flat and smooth. With a renewed sense of purpose, he paced the steps of a perfect length and run-up. Satisfied, he began his new routine: a few limbering up exercises, two or three press-ups, a deep breath, and begin.

First ball, a miss, the crate was untouched. Second ball, not much better. One more try to hit the bloody thing before he'd have to walk over to retrieve the balls. Another miss.

When the score reached just one strike from eighteen balls, a dejected Freddie took a break and sloped back to the tractor.

'Hey there, calling it a day?'

Freddie's head shot up, the voice was coming from the shadiest part of the pavilion decking where the silhouette of a man was waving to him.

'Eh?'

Never the sharpest knife in the kitchen, Freddie was always, for all his slow ways, unfailingly polite. Now he strode over to the dark figure, a ready smile spreading across his broad face.

'You're early for the practice nets, the lads aren't meeting up 'till after work. Do I know you? I'm Freddie, I am. Who are you?'

'Jacob. Pleased to meet you Freddie, I was just looking around the place…nice set-up you have here.'

'You play for Larchester? Been spying out the land 'ave you?'

Jacob threw his head back in amusement and stepped out from the shadows and on towards the newly cut cricket square. Freddie, unsure at first, followed behind, though he had no idea why.

'You've done a great job, the pitch looks good, that's a lovely looking wicket, Freddie.'

'Thanks.'

'You look like you're used to a good day's hard work, am I right?'

Freddie nodded vigorously.

'Yeah. I'm a slaughter man. That's me. What do you do…Jacob?'

'Oh, a bit of this and a bit of that, you know?'

Freddie nodded again, keen to demonstrate familiarity with Jacob's current employment status, even though he had none.

'So tell me about this team of yours, Freddie.'

Freddie hung his head a little, tiny beads of sweat dripping from his chin and neck onto his shirt collar, 'It's not my team, not really, I just look after the ground and stuff like that.'

It was Jacob's turn to nod, 'So, you don't play for them, then? Only, I saw you doing some bowling over there by the boundary.'

'I'm useless. Anyhow, shouldn't go sneaking around watching folk. Bet you had a good laugh, didn't you? Useless I am, bloody useless. Not that it's any of your bloody business.'

'Now then, lad, don't take on. Show me your hands.'

For reasons Freddie could not figure out, he obeyed. He knew his wrists were thick and wide, the palms rough and firm. Not only that, the fingers and thumbs were large and capable of making strong fists.

'Tell you what Freddie, these are a pair of good hands, have you got a bat handy?' enquired Jacob, knowing the answer but enjoying the conversation.

Any compliment goes a long way with Freddie.

'I have a set of keys for the kit locker. I could get one if you like.'

Less than two minutes passed before Freddie skipped out from the pavilion with a bat tucked under his arm.

'Right then Freddie, lad. Deep breath. I've got some bad news and some good news, alright?'

Freddie's huge right hand gripped the handle of the bat and he gave it a defiant swing before handing it to Jacob, 'You what?'

'It's like this mate, you're never going to make it as a bowler. That's just the way it is. I'm sorry to say.'

Freddie looked down at his feet and chewed over this announcement before squaring up to Jacob, 'You didn't have to take the piss. That's not right. The lads around 'ere are all good lads, they like a bit of banter but we don't take the piss. Now, you can be on your way, pal, before I clock you one. You hear me? On your way.'

Jacob stood firm as Freddie's forefinger jabbed him in the chest, 'Freddie, listen to me. I said I had good news as well. Do you want to hear it or do you want to use those fists of yours? Your choice.'

Freddie somehow managed to contain his fury, only just, 'Go on then.'

Jacob warmed to the task in hand, 'You sure?'

'Yeah, give me the good news, but if you take the piss again, I'm warning you. The lads won't stand for it, they look after me and we stick together, we do.'

'So they should. Right then. Get hold of this bat…here, not like that, like this…see? I'm going to fetch that old crate over and then I'll bowl a few at you and you're going to hit the ball as hard as you can.'

'Hang on, hang on, not so quick mister, are you listening to me, or what? I told you…'

'Oh, before we start, I nearly forgot…the good news.'

Freddie fists clenched around the bat.

'You'll never make a bowler, but we just might make a batsman out of you.'

'Nah.'

Jacob tossed the ball from one hand to the other and waited, 'So do you want to give it a try?'

The first two balls flew past Freddie's legs and thumped against the crate.

'Hold the bat straight, grip it like you saw me doing it just now and keep your head still, watch the ball.'

Freddie's face was hot and angry, creased with concentration. When the third ball struck his bat, the sound was solid, almost sweet, as it took flight over Jacob's head towards the pavilion roof. The next two were dispatched in similar style until Freddie's grimace was replaced with a beaming grin.

'Oh, and one more tip for you, Freddie, my friend. When you play, and you will play, always remember to concentrate hard before each over.'

'Aye, right. Reckon I'll do that. Mind you, that's never been a strong point with me. I'm not clever like, that way.'

Jacob seemed to anticipate this remark, 'Alright, well, try this then. Say to yourself, over and over in your head the same word. It'll help you keep your mind on what you're doing.'

'What word?'

He reached into his pocket for an envelope, 'I've written it down, so you don't forget it. Keep this safe, Freddie. The word is 'TOCONOM.'

CHAPTER FOUR

Judith Balfour thought she had died and gone to heaven. It seemed like yesterday that everything in her world had been blown to the four winds, but it felt now that all the fragments of her life had fallen back to earth in exactly the right place. She had always been a country girl at heart and always known that she wanted to be a teacher. But this? To become a head at such a young age was just the icing on the cake. This little school, in the very centre of Clamford with such a warm, friendly community, was everything she dreamed it would be.

This was almost the end of her second term in charge. It's gone so quickly. She doesn't want it to end, but the long summer break will be an opportunity to take stock and reflect. Perhaps she could allow herself a little self-congratulation, and a cup of coffee. Her staff were unfailingly supportive and enthusiastic, the children polite on the whole, the parents appreciative. All was as it should be.

The school building had gradually contracted over many years. Today, there was only one corridor in the building and it was short and narrow, with two classrooms and a tiny assembly area. This arrangement allowed Judith to keep close tabs on everything that went on; in fact, when she stood with her ear to the office door, she could almost hear individual voices as they laughed, cried, shouted and sang their way through the days.

This morning was a little unusual, one voice was cutting through the calm. It was undeniably persistent and impossible to ignore, yet Judith gripped her coffee mug even tighter and tried to dismiss it. It was impossible to suppress the nagging flutters in her stomach as the shrieks of little voices grew in number and volume.

A knock on the door made her jump.

'Judith, I think you'd better come and see for yourself. Oscar's escaped, Hilda is leading the rebellion.'

'Ah, Hilda,' sighed Judith.

If there was the tiniest of clouds hovering above Judith's blue horizon, they were embodied in the diminutive figure of this precocious child; six going on sixteen, beloved adopted daughter of the Reverend Geoffrey Roper and his wife, Julia. Despite the frequent tantrums, and stubborn resistance to authority figures, she still felt a smidgeon of sympathy towards the vicar's young daughter. Hilda was a plain child who would, in all probability, grow into a plain woman. Judith understood such unspoken matters and consoled herself with the thought that Hilda had a few years to go before she realised the sad truth.

A stampede of children was trying to force its way along through the doors at the end of the corridor while Katy, the junior staff member, stood at the threshold, arms and legs outstretched like Leonardo's Vitruvian man.

'Someone must have opened the latch; he can't have gone far. I know what we'll do. Katy, I'll take Hilda and a couple of others with me, you and Maureen keep the others inside. Distract them, sing, play, whatever, but do NOT let them outside. We'll find him, I'm sure.'

Once outside, Hilda's small, freckled face glowered suspiciously up at Judith.

'He could be miles away by now. It's your fault, you're supposed to look after us.'

'No, Hilda, we'll find him. He's probably hiding under a bush.'

'You don't know that. He could be anywhere.'

The two boys dashed off to the edge of the little playground to rummage around the bushes, while Judith led Hilda towards the path at the side of the building. The search was still in its infancy when, out on the main road by the village square, the unfamiliar screech of brakes could be heard.

Now, her heart was thumping in her chest. A door slammed, and a man's voice roared around the square with terrifying ferocity. She grabbed Hilda by the hand and called over to the two boys, trying, in vain, to stop her brain from conjuring up a dozen or more chilling images of a prone Oscar beneath the wheels of a van. Slowly, the little group shuffled towards the school gates.

Snowy Elstrop was in no mood for introductions. He hadn't stepped foot in the school for decades and had no idea who the new headmistress was, and cared even less. Face a mask of fury, he didn't wait to draw breath.

'Somebody is going to compensate me for any damage to my goods, I hope you know that, missus. Took me hours to stack it all up in the back of the van, I doesn't dare look to see what a mess it's in now. I thought it was one of them little terrier things running out into t'road. Damned thing came out of nowhere. If I'd known it was a bloody rabbit, I'd have driven over it.'

Hilda slipped her hand from Judith's grip before she could be restrained and dashed forward.

'You are horrible!' she bawled.

Oscar lay still, on his side, eyes shut. One of the boys was on the verge of tears, so Judith began to usher the children away when, from nowhere, a shadow cast its shape over the prone rabbit.

'Hello. My name's Jacob. Can I take a look at him? Is that alright?'

Jacob didn't wait for a reply and gently rested his right hand against Oscar's furry neck, while Snowy pulled a face.

'I reckon it's a dead'un. Best shovel it away.'

Hilda kicked Snowy in the shin.

'Shut up! Shut up! Horrible man. Go away, I hope you die!'

Judith grabbed Hilda by the shoulders and heaved her away from Snowy who gave a casual shrug, a thin smirk appearing on his ruddy face.

Jacob was hunched over the rabbit, to allow his hand to trace its gentle way over the fur, while he stroked its ears and lowered his face as if to whisper to the poor thing.

'Still breathing, can't feel anything broken. Could be it's just in shock and stunned.'

He put his mouth close to Oscar's whiskers and breathed hard, then whispered again.

The rabbit's eyes opened, but it didn't move. Jacob stroked the fur once more and continued to whisper under his breath.

Suddenly, Oscar moved his head, then his paws. Jacob smiled up at Hilda.

'What's your name?'

'Hilda. That's Oscar, he's our rabbit. We keep him in a hutch. What's yours?'

'Jacob. Pleased to meet you. Can you help me please, Hilda? Just put your hands underneath Oscar and gently lift him up…with me…after three…that's it. Let's take him back where he's safe…that's it.'

Judith and the two boys trailed behind Hilda and Jacob. By the time they reached Oscar's hutch, Snowy Elstrop's van had already disappeared from the square.

'Is he going to be alright, Jacob?'

Oscar sniffed and hopped his way around his hutch, blinking occasionally at the children as they huddled around.

'He'll be fine. You need a better latch on his door, keep an eye on him, change his food and water and he'll be as right as rain.'

Hilda threw her arms around Jacob's legs and hugged them.

'Thank you, thank you.'

Judith felt the relief flow down through her neck and shoulders.

'I am indebted to you, and I'll take your advice about a new latch.'

Hilda let go of Jacob's legs, her face inquisitive and slightly flushed.

'Mister Jacob, what did you whisper in Oscar's ear?'

Jacob knelt and shared his secret. Hilda nodded twice, satisfied.

It was lunchtime before Judith could fully regain her powers of concentration sufficiently enough to plan for the end of term concert for the children. On her desk was a half-finished mug of coffee and the unopened envelope that Jacob had shoved in her hand. She was sure it would contain his contact number in case there were odd jobs to be done. People who live in villages always seem to do that, offering services for odd-jobbing but, these days, there's vetting and security to think about where children are concerned. Stick to the rules, girl.

She sighed and stepped out into the corridor passage; the children had had their lunch, and some were heading out to the tiny playground with Katy leading the way. Among them was Hilda, head erect, smiling.

'TOCONOM, TOCONOM, TOCONOM,' the little girl sang.

CHAPTER FIVE

Ted Smailes was known as a beer man, rarely touching spirits and never one to mix the grape with the grain but, today, he ordered a gin and tonic. To his surprise, he enjoyed it.

The Fox and Grape was filling with a few regulars and some casual visitors who popped in for a quick pub lunch before moving on.

'Don't see so much of you these days Ted, is Doris keeping you on a tight leash?'

'Huh! She tries bless her.'

Sandra Hewitt decided not to pursue this line any further, content to let sleeping dogs lie, though she' would have loved to know more about the new tenant who had moved into the cottage that Ted bought from Marcia Bennett. Patience and discretion, they were the keys to uncovering a good tale or a juicy piece of gossip; years behind the bar serving customers had taught her well. For now, she'd leave Ted alone with his thoughts and his gin and tonic. This was certainly not the old Ted, everybody could see that. Nevertheless, it was good to have him back on a lunchtime session.

The door swung open and Snowy Elstrop, eyes like thunder, headed straight for the far end by the dartboard, where Sandra's husband Len was already reaching for a pint glass in which to pour Snowy's pint of bitter.

'Len, you wouldn't bloody credit it would'yer?'

'Hey up! Somebody's rattled your cage.'

'Bloody rabbit, right in front of my van. I'll have to park up and reload.'

'After you've downed your pint.'

'Too bloody right.'

Ted carried his gin and tonic along the bar where Snowy greeted him with a curt nod.

'Come off it, Snowy! Who are you kidding? When have you ever sorted out that old death trap?'

Snowy was ready to take the bait.

Old instincts die hard, Ted braced himself, whispering under his breath, ready to swing away from the other man's fists should the need arise, incapable of disguising the dancing mischief of his eyes nor the little crease marks at the side of his jovial, whiskered face.

Whispering again, Ted turned to face Snowy full on and immediately sensed in the man a slow gathering of calm purpose. Len watched the long pause, his hand still gripped around the freshly pulled pint.

At last Snowy spoke, 'You're lucky I haven't clocked you one, Ted Smailes.'

Another pause, then Ted's laughter broke the ice and Snowy was left almost breathless with hysteria at the absurdity of his anger.

Ted reached into his pocket for his wallet and nodded to Len.

'Just a tonic this time, to top up my gin.'

Snowy's hand grasped Ted's arm, 'Put that away lad, I'll get this. You were right an'all, I've been meaning to get rid of the old van for weeks but I 'aven't got around to it. My Ethel keeps banging on at me about it.'

'Time for a change then, Ruddick's garage at Larchester will see you right, they had a decent wagon on the forecourt last week, few years old but in good nick. Give them a try.'

'Aye, reckon it's time I did.'

Sandra looked at her watch, she would have to call time in ten minutes. She must have been watching this little scene for longer than she thought, her right leg had gone stiff. Something was going on around this place and yet she couldn't put her finger on it. It wasn't like her. It felt good, whatever it was, calming and restful. Ted Smailes quaffing gin and tonics; Snowy Elstrop backing down from a ruck. Something was definitely happening. She left the bar to go upstairs to the bathroom. The cool water on her face was soothing, but the air was too warm and stuffy up there so she nipped along the landing to the front bedroom. Her vaping device was where she left it by the bed, but she felt no compunction to use it. She reached for the sash window latch and let in some air. Immediately, her eyes were drawn down below to where Jacob was crossing the road on his way back to his cottage. He was whistling, hands in pocket, but he didn't look up. She watched him carefully as her lips parted a little and her fingers went to her throat. She smiled as he disappeared. So that was him, was it?

When Sandra returned to the bar, Ted was about to leave, 'Don't leave it so long, Ted. Good to see you enjoying yourself.'

'You can count on it, Sandra.'

He called over to Snowy, 'Let me know if you want me go with you to look at vans.'

'Yeah? Will you come with me, Ted?'

'Well aye lad. Just say the word.'

CHAPTER SIX

It looked like rain was on the way, Peggy Sudron tried to find something to smile about but it was no use, her shoulders stiffened. Knuckles showing white beneath her skin, she gripped the handles of her husband's wheelchair and quickened her pace.

'That's all we need.'

Recently, she acquired the habit of grinding her teeth. It usually happened when she was tired or just plain irritated and angry. She knew that she was doing it now.

'Just a bit further.'

They reached the west end of the village, yards from the gate to Smailes's farm opposite the entrance to the drive leading to Brompton Hall. Both these locations would certainly greet them with a sympathetic welcome, but…

'No, Jim, I have to get the tea on, and if we get soaked, it'll be me who has to dry everything off. I left the brolly in the kitchen, never thought it would turn to rain, you should have reminded me.'

'My fault again, eh?'

Despite her mood, she secretly harboured the hope that her husband's condition would continue to improve. This time last year, she reminded herself, he could barely make himself understood to anyone except the family...and Camilla, of course. Camilla. She was almost family now.

Peggy pictured the scene at Brompton Hall. Camilla would probably arrange for tea and sandwiches while their son, Roy, hovered somewhere in the background. He would want to show them he was familiar and relaxed with the splendid surroundings of course. And he'd allow his lover to take the lead while she entertained his parents. That would be alright, Jim loved it at Brompton and was genuinely fond of Camilla.

Peggy, on the other hand, had yet to fully overcome the awkward embarrassment of such a socially sensitive issue.

The clouds thickened overhead, and a few drops of rain hit the pavement.

Peggy swivelled and pivoted the wheelchair in a u-turn, determined to head for home. Only she fully understood the truth of it. Jim might not improve. In fact, this was probably as good as it would get. She would suppress such thoughts for as long as she could, just as she had done every day for the past few months. Those endless hours when she would cling to the handles of the wheelchair, looking at the back of her husband's ageing head, alone in her world. Pounding the pavement, nodding at passers-by, resenting Jim's infirmity, his helplessness, the bath washing, the dressing and undressing, cleaning up after his mess. The worst moments were when he seemed to enjoy all the fuss. That wasn't her Jim, the old Jim. Everything had changed, and she hated it.

They had only gone a few yards more when they heard heavy boot steps, from behind.

'Hello there, you're going to get soaked, let me help.'

'No thank you, we're fine.'

'I've got an umbrella and you can drape my jacket over his knees if you like.'

Jim said nothing, but raised a thumb of approval.

'My name's Jacob. I was just walking my horse, Joey, at Smailes's farm when I spotted you by the gate. I had a quick word with Doris and grabbed the brolly. It's ok. Let me help, can't have you getting drenched.'

'Very kind of you, I'm sure. This is Jim and I'm Peggy.'

Jacob held the brolly high while Peggy pushed on. The conversation meandered through some local trivia, before Peggy took a breath and slowed the pace.

'I did hear something about you and your horse.'

'You did, eh? Who from?'

'Oh well, I don't quite recall.'

Jim raised an arm, 'I bet it was Doris!'.

Peggy floundered for a few moments until Jacob noticed the first undeniable flash of laughter in her eyes.

'Aye. Thought as much. Well then, Peggy, that makes a difference, doesn't it? What you hear depends on who's doing the talking, that's what I reckon, anyhow.'

Peggy looked at him straight for the first time, his eyes had no mischief and they possessed no malice when he laughed.

For a moment, her blank face was soft, vulnerable, and free of pain.

'I'll take a turn if you like…pushing?'

She stepped aside to let him take over and smiled, despite herself.

By the time they arrived at the farm gate, the rain had dwindled to a few spots. Last Autumn, the Sudron boys built a wooden ramp at the back door to the kitchen, making it much easier to get the wheelchair inside.

The room is warm and airless, so Peggy opens a couple of windows.

'We used to have Tan, our border collie, he'd lie on the sill, right here, but he was an old dog and we lost him last year. I did think of getting another one, a pup, but not yet. I have too much on my plate with Jim…and Roy's not around much for walking dogs, these days. You'll have a cup of tea?'

'That's kind, thank you, if it's no trouble.'

'If you can help Jim into the front room, there's a hand rail he can use, I'll pop the kettle on.'

The house was pretty much as Jacob imagined it might be: the white sink, the low beams, the large table and welsh dresser. Perhaps, he hadn't reckoned on an upright piano in the front room, but the two sofas, open fireplace, family pictures and low oak tables came as no great surprise. Neither did the radio and the boxes of pills nor the commode in the corner.

'We manage ok. I... don't use that bloody... commode thing...much, these days... have my physio twice a week but... I'm getting there...'ere... sit yourself down, lad.'

He hadn't expected that. The clarity of Jim's voice, despite the faltering hesitancy, was firm and deep. It was as if the old man was hoping for a reaction. The thought made Jacob chuckle.

'Speech therapy...on Fridays.'

'Ah! That's good. Can't be easy for you both.'

'She's a good'un...my Peg.'

Jacob decided not to attempt a new a conversation, content to allow his respect for Jim's simple dignity to reveal itself through silence. Eventually, the quiet of the farmhouse was broken by the sound of the boiling kettle from the kitchen.

'She...likes a...bit of company... my Peg.'

Jacob hesitated, but the urge was too strong.

'Yes, I know she does.'

In the kitchen, Peggy sang to herself a little tune she picked up on Jim's radio; she had no idea what it was called, but it was catchy and, right now, she couldn't get it out of her head. Their wet things were drying nicely in the warmth, so no harm was done. Tomorrow, she'd return Doris's brolly, that'd fill an hour. She fetched a tray from the dresser and reached past Camilla's mug to wash some fresh ones. She could hear the two men chatting away in the front room and the sound made her pause and smile before she could bring herself to disturb the talking with the tea and biscuits. She smiled at them both.

The conversation was sluggish, but light and easy. It' had been just a few days, but the village was more familiar to Jacob now: the names and faces, the houses.

After half an hour, he left the Sudrons to their late afternoon routines. The sun was returning and lengthening shadows appeared on the pavement. A ginger cat crossed his path, otherwise it was quiet in Clamford as he reached his cottage.

Back in the farmhouse Peggy cleared away the pots and watched from the kitchen window as her youngest, Kenny, brought the tractor into the yard. In the front room, Jim's eyes were closed in concentration as he repeated the word that Jacob suggested he employ as part of his therapy.

CHAPTER SEVEN

Julia had waited for half an hour until the right moment arrived; even now, she was not sure this was it, 'Hilda, darling, come here a moment.'

'Toconom, toconom, toconom.'

'Hilly…here…now!'

Hilda thrust her fists into her sides and glowered at her mother, Julia, 'I am in the middle of playing something.'

The vicarage garden came into its own at this time of year, especially the borders where the Ropers had carefully planned the planting to ensure a long summer of constant colour. Under the shade of an old parasol, Julia watched her children. How could anyone begin to think of giving away such beautiful children? What dreadful circumstances must have driven the parents to such a tortuous decision? They were so different, these little people who filled her life to the brim with such contentment and joy. Aidan, the quiet little boy with the mischievous streak and Hilda, his big bossy boots of a sister. Aidan's red pedal car was abandoned to the shed these days, outgrown and ready for the parish jumble sale. Climbing trees and kicking a plastic ball were his current pleasures. Of course, there was no biological reason the two children should bear any resemblance to each other and yet, Julia often noticed a touching, protective bond between them. It moved and delighted her.

Aidan tensed a little as his mother summonsed Hilda to her side, one more time. At last, she obeyed and stomped towards the parasol. Relieved and deep inside his thoughts, he stared down at his football, deep in thought, and gave it a mighty punt into the rhododendron bushes. Julia calculated it would probably take him ten minutes to retrieve it, which would give her enough time to engage properly with her stubborn daughter.

'What were you playing?'

'A game...I told you.'

'Yes, but what sort of game?'

'A dancing game.'

'Oh, I see, do you like dancing?'

'Don't know, I just thought it was a good idea because I'm so hot.'

Julia took Hilda's hand, it was damp with sweat.

'Have some lemon barley, it will make you feel better. Why did you think that dancing around in the warm sun would cool you down? Silly girl.'

Hilda swigged back some lemon barley and wiped the back of her arm across her mouth.

'Dancing is not silly, not if it works.'

Julia surrendered to laughter.

'How can it make you cooler, silly billy?'

'Well, if it rains, we'll get cold and wet. Then we won't be warm. But, if we were dancing before the rain came, we'd be ready and nice and warm, see?'

'Ah! Right. So… it was a rain dance?'

Hilda shrugged her shoulders and took another swig of lemon barley.

'And what were you chanting?'

'What's chanting?'

'What were you singing?'

'I wasn't singing.'

'Saying then, what were you saying over and over? I heard you; you were saying something when you were dancing, what was it?'

'A magic word.'

'A magic word, I see, to make it rain.'

Hilda nodded slowly, her eyes closing for a couple of seconds while she thought of something to say to convince her mother of the obvious logic of her actions.

'Well, it worked for Oscar.'

'Who is Oscar?'

'At school.'

Julia frowned, she and Geoffrey reckoned they knew most of the families in Clamford by now, this was a new name. If there had been a baptism at St Barnabas's, she'd have remembered, Oscar was a name she wouldn't forget.

'Oscar. Is he a friend of yours?'

Hilda, exasperated, was approaching snapping point, Julia recognised the signs, and they filled her with trepidation. Time to move things along with caution. Yes, this was a moment for calm patience and self-discipline.

'Mummy! Oscar! The rabbit!'

Julia made her voice as soft and gentle as she could manage.

'Of course. Oscar…'

'Jacob said the magic word and Oscar came alive again. Miss Balfour saw it as well.'

'What do you mean…he came alive again?'

Hilda folded her arms and her mother rubbed a tiny piece of grass from the child's cheek.

'Oscar was lying in the road, dead, and he came alive again. I told you; Jacob said the magic word.'

'The same word you were saying just now?'

Hilda nodded, 'Just like in the story, like Jesus. Oscar is like Jesus. Magic, see? And I say it might work for rain, only it hasn't yet but it will, you'll see. Can I play now, Mummy? Please?'

'Five more minutes, and find your brother.'

Julia leaned back in her chair beneath the parasol. Tonight, when the children were in bed, she must speak to Geoffrey about this.

CHAPTER EIGHT

The Reverend Peter Stephenson was in a cheerful mood. A new piece of gossip was flying around Clamford and there was nothing he enjoyed more than juicy gossip. Gossip, he told himself, was an essential element of the glue mixture that bound communities together...don't knock it. It was now over two years since his arrival as the young curate of St Barnabas's and he still couldn't believe his good fortune. He'd expected and hoped for a challenging inner-city parish, but had been fully prepared to accept the hand he was dealt, wherever it took him. The timing had been perfect. To arrive in this curious village just when Harriet Wilberforce unleashed her bombshell, her notorious legacy, was most fortuitous. Many times, he had gazed up at her brazen statue in a state of thankful devotion, refreshed and re-energized for the days ahead. Not only that, in the vicar, Geoffrey Roper, he had found a wise and patient mentor.

Yesterday, Peter caught sight of a single grey hair emerging from his thick beard. He managed to make it disappear with an old pair of kitchen scissors, but the experience left him a little flat. Should he shave away his pride and joy? The lads in the cricket team and the Fox and Grape would have his life if he went clean shaven but...he spent less time these days in the pub and, in any case, they'd soon tire and get used to his new look. He would decide over the weekend.

Today was a brighter day. He flicked through the jackets, shirts and trousers hanging from the wobbling clothes rail in his bedroom. This was not a day for rugby tops and jeans. Fridays were for pastoral visits. Today, Peter would make his fortnightly pilgrimage to Ramsden House, the posh care home on the outskirts of Larchester, to pay a call on dear old Marcia Bennett. Such a pleasant old soul, she was an intelligent lady who would still occupy the cottage a couple of doors down the street if it hadn't been for that nasty fall, last year. The people at Ramsden House were very good, they owned a minibus to take residents to the local garden centre on Tuesday mornings and, sometimes, to the coast. On Sunday mornings, Marcia was always brought to the church, along with a few others who came for the ride.

Marcia always welcomed Peter into her own private room, never in the residents' lounge. He was very familiar with her room, with its fragrance of lily of the valley, old magazines and the ancient framed photograph of the priest by her bed. The ritual didn't change: she would beckon him to sit next to the coffee table while she took the armchair by the window so that she could observe who came and went. After a few minutes of polite chat, mainly regarding her health and welfare, there would be a knock at the door and Jane Simpson, the young care manager of Ramsden House, would enter with a tray of tea and biscuits. The refreshments were always welcome, of course, but it was Jane who provided the distraction that Peter most enjoyed. Blonde and gregarious, the ultimate professional, she seemed to glide around the rooms as if on wheels, eyes sparkling with good health and vitality.

'I'll pop in for a quick chat, before I go, if that's ok, Jane.'

'Yes, of course, see you later, enjoy your tea and biscuits.'

Then, the ritual demanded that it be time to update Marcia with the parish news.

'There's not a lot to tell you about, really, except for one bit of news which will interest you. Apparently, Ted Smailes has found a tenant for the cottage. A chap called Jacob.'

'Oh… I did wonder if…sorry…do go on.'

She glanced out, unseeing, through the window.

'To be honest, I don't know much about it but, last night, a few of the lads were saying that he has moved in, just for a short-term arrangement.'

'I see, how interesting.'

Suddenly, her voice could belong to Agatha Christie's Miss Marple, but Peter resisted the urge to smile.

'Seems a decent chap.'

'You've met him then?'

'No, not yet, just going by what I've been hearing. Seems to have created his own little fan club. If it's the same fellow, I think he's walked past my window a couple of times…tall, carries himself well. I expect we'll bump into each other at some point and I'll be able to tell you more.'

Marcia drained her cup of tea and placed her hands in her lap, 'It's rather fortunate that this gentleman has arrived when the weather is fine. The heating can be tricky in the winter if you don't know what you're doing.'

This was the signal to wind the conversation down to a natural conclusion. He left her with a gentle kiss to the cheek and made his way down the passage to Jane Simpson's office.

Jane's smile had a beguiling openness which reminded him of a girl in his junior school, when he was growing up in Manchester. There was no sense of defiance in those eyes, they were gentle yet strong, vulnerable yet resilient; Peter could easily drown in them.

'Oh no thanks, I've had enough tea for one day, Jane. I just wanted to do my usual check-in with you. All seems well with Marcia?'

'I would say so, she's a real dear. Her confidence is coming back, she can walk around the gardens with her stick. Of course, we make sure there's always someone there to support her.'

'Yes, she was telling me. I'm glad it seems to be working out…I had to break the news that her old cottage has been let. I thought it might upset her, but she seemed ok with it. She went quiet, but she's a quiet soul, isn't she?'

'Ah. I'll tell the staff to keep a close eye on her this week. Sometimes people take it badly if they feel the last links with their old life are disappearing into history.'

Peter nodded in agreement. He would love to discover much, much, more about this wise beauty: her ambitions, her thoughts and ideas, her desires. He wanted to sit down and chat for a while but felt himself suddenly rooted to the spot, tense and stiff.

'I wonder, Jane, if I may ask you a question.'

'Shoot.'

'It's a personal one, is that alright?'

'Okay…'

'Do you think I should shave off my beard?'

'Hmm, no I think it suits you. Besides, curates need a bit of gravitas, don't they? Keep it.'

'Right.'

'Was that it?'

'Eh? Oh yeah…I mean, not really, I have another question.'

'Go on then, Fire away.'

'Well, Marcia's old cottage is only a few doors from mine, they're very similar properties. I wondered if you'd like to come over, some time, to see it…get a better idea…maybe…'

'That's not a personal question. An invitation to view a property.'

'It is…in a way…I mean…Oh God… God…this is so… the question is really…'

'My word! If it takes the power of prayer to ask it, then it must be a very heavy question.'

Her eyes were dancing with playfulness and she laughed, loud, her teeth flashing, unafraid.

'You're teasing me, aren't you?'

'Yes, I am. If it'll help…if you are asking me to come on a date to your cottage in Clamford, then the answer is YES. If that wasn't the question, get lost!'

'It was, bang on, the question.'

'That's ok then. I'm free this weekend.'

CHAPTER NINE

It was Saturday already, and less than a week since Jacob arrived with Joey, his faithful piebald. The shade of the old stable block among the Smailes's outbuildings was cooling as he stroked the old horse's mane and observed it feeding on a handful of oats.

'You're looking so much better, my friend. So much better.'

He gave Joey an extra rub along his neck and strode out into the sun. The Smailes boys were in the fields somewhere, he could hear them laughing and shouting to each other, while Doris and Ted were in their kitchen. The door was open to let in some air.

Jacob hovered in the yard.

'Well, he's no trouble, I'll give you that, Ted.'

'I told you, he's a decent guy.'

'I suppose the extra money's handy 'till you get sorted with a permanent arrangement. Do you think he'll be staying much longer?'

'How should I know, woman? He said it would be for a short stay, so I expect that'll be the way of it.'

'Talk of the village, yesterday, it was.'

'How do you mean?'

'In Millers shop, Cynthia Pearson and Audrey Waterhouse were all ears.'

'No change there, then…'

'Joan and Cissie were telling the tale…you know…about Joan's shoulder, or was it her back? Anyway, that's not important, the thing is that Judith Balfour had been in the day before and she had another tale to tell…are you listening Ted or am I talking to myself?'

'About the rabbit, you mean?'

'Aye, how do you know about that?'

'From Snowy Elstrop.'

'You never said.'

'You never asked.'

Doris stood up and twisted around abruptly, 'Aye, well, seems our Jacob's a bit of a pin-up around here, suddenly.'

She began to giggle, which set Ted off until he almost choked on his tea, 'Give over, woman!'

Outside in the yard, Jacob listened to the silence and smiled at the sound of such warm affection and close intimacy, a sound he hadn't heard for a long time.

Leaving the farm through the main gates, he was immediately distracted by a breeze way up as it meandered through the tops

of the trees behind the twin portals at the entrance to Brompton
Hall. The main gates remained open as usual, just as they had
been every day since he arrived in Clamford. Curiosity
prompted his footsteps forward past them, through to the drive.
The tree-lined avenue was alive with birdsong and he slowed his
pace at the first bend to listen until he felt a presence at his
elbow.

'Oh, sorry Miss, I didn't hear you.'

'You weren't meant to.'

Jacob stopped in his tracks. The young woman was tall and
striking, her dark hair loose at her shoulders. She slid her
sunglasses up her brow to rest on top of her head, her eyes were
cautious but not accusing, her tone neutral.

'You have business at Brompton?'

She did not say Hall.

'Could be I have.'

She scrutinised him, carefully, for a few seconds.

'Let me guess…you're looking for work, right?'

'You reckon?'

Her laugh betrayed absolutely nothing; her voice was steady,
unafraid.

'I'll walk there with you, come on.'

At her side, Jacob could smell her perfume, spicy but cool, expensive. Now he knew who she was.

They walked without a word for a few yards until the Hall came into view, grand but not imposing or forbidding, casting a broad rectangle of shadow across the lawns. A Land Rover was parked under an oak, but there was no one to be seen. The air was still full and heavy with the noise of birds and insects and Jacob could hear the flow of the river, somewhere over the bushes and trees. His gaze followed the thin gravel path as it wound around the edge of the lawns towards the rear of Brompton Hall.

'What sort of work do you do?'

'Oh. I can turn my hand to most things.'

She knew she believed him in an instant. There was something in the way he spoke and moved, that must be it: neutral, not shy but simple, matter of fact, almost tranquil, rooted deep in truth.

'I'll show you around…if you like.'

'Thank you, that's kind.'

The sound of gravel beneath their feet broke the next little silence.

'I'm Camilla Wilberforce…I live…'

'Here, yes, I know. I am Jacob.'

'I guessed as much.'

They stopped.

'How did you guess?'

'You're the talk of the village.'

She expected him to laugh off her words, perhaps with a shrug, possibly a self-deprecating grin, but he simply nodded at her.

At the rear of the Hall, the path split several ways through the gardens, as she chose one of them and resumed, 'It's Saturday, it's quiet today but, through the week, this place gets busy with gardeners. Many of them are locals, as you can see there's plenty of land for fruit, vegetables, everything.'

'Aye, looks good.'

In the middle distance, among the rows of potatoes and cabbages, two men were chatting. One of them waved over at Camilla while his friend doffed his cap.

'Those two are regulars here, come over, I'll introduce you.'

The two men leaned on their spades as Camilla led Jacob through the vegetable plots.

'This is Jacob. Jacob, this is Trevor, he keeps an allotment near to here, and this chap is Fred who's getting on a bit and likes to come down here just for the fun of it, don't you, Fred?'

The older man smiled and nodded and reached out to shake Jacob's hand, 'I do that, Ma'am it helps to keep me moving.'

Trevor followed suit, his grip was firm, he was stripped to the waist, tattoos stark and vivid in the afternoon sun.

Camilla pointed to an area just a few yards away where a scarecrow leaned awkwardly on his pole, 'And this is Arthur! We brought Arthur here from the allotments I told you of. He's useless as a scarecrow, but he has sentimental value.'

Looking at her more closely now, Jacob could see that, here in this quiet place, she was younger than he imagined. The dark hair was careless and loose, the mouth a little wider, the smile warmer. She was not looking at Arthur, he noticed, but somewhere in space, and her posture was completely relaxed. He turned his head away from her to scan the far wall towards a couple of greenhouses and, in deep shade, a large shed. Closer to the wall, the river could be heard clearly on the other side. A bicycle was propped up against the shed.

'Trevor's bike. He's a good lad. Helped me a lot.'

Jacob opened the shed door and peered inside.

'There's a switch to your left.'

He found it and blinked hard as the shed tried to come to life in the dimness.

Tattoo Trevor hovered at the door, Fred at his side.

'Somebody must have had the idea of putting a power line in, probably years ago. We keep the lawn mowers and tools in here. The potting bench is alright, it's sturdy enough and right over in the corner there's a workbench but you can't see it properly in this lot. Nobody's used it since we don't know when. Probably loads of stuff hidden away over the years. I've never had a good look to be honest with you. Prefer to be outside.'

'Needs a bit of a tidy up, that's all. The shed itself is sturdy enough, and the roof is good.'

Jacob smiled and switched off the light, 'Tell you what. Give me a week. I'll sort out the shed, get it all working right and fix that wall over there and sort out that raised bed over by the corner. If you think I've made a decent fist of it, then pay me what you think it's worth. If you're not happy, I'll be on my way…no hard feelings.'

Camilla nodded her approval, 'Ok you're on. And don't mind Snowy Elstrop, his bark is worse than his bite. He and his wife, Ethel, are in charge of cleaning and general work around the house and gardens. He thinks he's more important than he really is, so does Ethel, but they're both good workers in their own way. My aunt hired them quite a few years ago, so I've just kept the arrangement going.'

'I reckon I know how to handle Snowy.'

'Yes, I reckon you probably do.'

Fred retreated to tend to a vine that was creeping along the warm bricks of the wall, his fingers gently traced its branches and leaves.

Jacob watched on, 'How long have you been helping here, Fred?'

'It sometimes feels like forever…and a bit more.'

Jacob laughed and tapped the old man on the shoulder, 'Well, that's grand. An old- fashioned gardener, I like to see that. I bet you talk to the plants. I do it all the time. Plants and animals.'

Fred chuckled, 'I do that, lad.'

Jacob leaned in towards the vine and brushed his hand against the thickest of the branches, whispering to the plants as Fred stood back, transfixed.

'Toconom, toconom.'

CHAPTER TEN

The Roper family's large kitchen at Saint Barnabas's vicarage faced north and was pleasantly cool in the early afternoon until the sun moved around.

'I've bought most of the things I might need, that's to say I don't think I've forgotten anything. The Millers were very helpful. So, what do you reckon, Julia, curry or pasta? Help me out here.'

Julia had one eye on the garden where young Aidan was perilously close to the blackberry bushes. She topped up her green tea and returned to the kitchen table where Peter Stephenson leaned back expectantly.

'Why on earth didn't you ask the poor girl what her preferences are?'

He shrugged off the question and took a gulped down the last of his can of cola, 'My culinary prowess doesn't extend very far but I've been practicing on a few things. No, no honestly, and curry and pasta are my best options I think.'

'Pasta then.'

'Thanks, that's what I thought. You're a star. I need to be pushing off soon, how long do you think Geoff is going to be?'

'Not much longer, it's just that he's a bit troubled about Hilda and he wants to have ten minutes with her, on her own, no distractions…to set her right, I suppose.'

Peter grinned, 'Right, well, good luck with that.'

'Well quite but, all the same, he's got a point.'

It was one of Peter's strengths he could spin his attention away from the slightly frivolous to the more pressing and serious issues of the day, with very little effort. At least, that's what he told himself.

'Hmm, Hilda's a very bright kid. I don't mean to be nosey, but there's nothing wrong is there? Nothing serious, I mean? You know I'd love to help if you think I can. Is there anything I can do?'

'Maybe. I suspect that's why he wants to chat with you.'

Upstairs, a door opened and the sound of small shoes thumping hard on the stairs filled the house. Julia shot straight to the window. To her relief, out on the lawn, brother and sister happily resumed their game of kickabout.

'She seems happy enough, thank goodness. Still, you never know, I'd better go outside and make sure all's well with them. Why don't you go up to the study now? If I don't see you before you go, hope your date goes well. Good luck with the pasta.'

The loud ticking of the grandfather clock at the top of the landing never failed to instil an air of quiet dignity, if not authority. There was a time, not so long ago, Peter recalled, when he would always pause to look at its sombre brass face and Roman numerals, then take a breath before entering Geoffrey's study. Not anymore.

Geoffrey was not behind his desk, he lay across a large bean bag, face raised to the ceiling, eyes closed. Peter offered a tiny cough and the vicar's eyes opened.

'Just give me a second or two, will you? There's a fresh bottle of water over there, grab a couple of glasses. It's suddenly very warm in here.'

Peter thought about reaching out his arm to assist Geoffrey to hoist himself up, the way footballers did it for their teammates on Match of the Day, instead, he headed for the water.

'I think daughters are exhausting. Ours certainly is. Boys are much easier.'

It was a full minute before Geoffrey could compose himself behind his desk.

'I think we may have a problem, Peter.'

Peter was about to taste the water when his hand stopped in mid- air, his face collapsed, unsure and still.

'Have I done something to…'

Geoffrey waved an arm and offered a rueful smile.

'No, not at all. Nothing like that. In fact, I've been meaning to say to you how much I've valued your work and friendship these past months. No…apologies if I've inferred otherwise. On the contrary, it's probably time to begin consideration of your next move. But that's for another day. No, it seems there may be a problem…in the village.'

The curate eased back in his seat. There were so many things he wanted to say. His destiny was here, the place he always dreamed of, where he comes alive. He wanted to explain how the excitement and magic of this strange little village had seeped its way into every fibre of his soul, as if it has chosen him, and not the other way around. But this was a moment intended for listening, he realised.

'How can I put this? It would seem we have a miracle worker in our midst, if we are to believe the local stories.'

'Can he change this water into wine, I wonder? I suddenly feel the need for alcohol.'

'What... can't get enough of the stuff, eh?'

'Ouch!'

'Oh... come on, Peter. Only pulling your leg. The Fox and Grape is a good place to keep tabs on what's going on, so long as one doesn't get too close to the gossipmongers. Have you heard anything about this fellow, Jacob...don't know his other name, renting Marcia Bennett's old cottage? How is she, by the way? Did you see her yesterday?'

Peter made his voice as cheerful as he could manage, hoping, perhaps, he could introduce the subject of Jane before Julia spilled the beans.

'Yes, I saw her. She has her good days. You know Marcia, she always puts on a brave face. Physically, she's slowed down a lot, but her walking has improved. She seems settled enough. Mind you, when I mentioned that someone had moved into her old cottage, she went quiet and flat but, on the whole, nothing to report really. I expect we'll see her tomorrow as usual.'

'That's good. Splendid place, Ramsden House. Anything else?'

Now was the moment.

'As a matter of fact…I don't know whether you recall the manager…of course you do…Jane. Well, anyway, the thing is, I've invited her over to my place this evening, just for a meal…thought you should know.'

Geoffrey's expression gave nothing away, 'I see, well thank you for informing me, anything else?'

This response was slightly unsettling, if not totally unexpected, and the best Peter could summon up in reply was a shake of the head.

'Good, well I might pop over to see Marcia myself at some point next week. Now, about the matter at hand.'

'The miracle worker. Well, it's only gossip, of course.'

Geoffrey frowned, determined not to lose his focus. He wanted to use expressions like keeping vigilant and nipping it in the bud, but this might be seen as heavy handedness and that would only make matters worse. A light touch…there he almost had it, but not quite, it smacked of trendy management speech. If he waited a moment or two longer, the right words would come.

'There's a bit more to it than just idle gossip, I fear.'

'Yeah?'

'Hilda has got it into her head that this Jacob fellow can raise people from the dead, like Jesus, she informed me, by using a magic word. Can you believe that? Ever since that incident at the school, with the rabbit, you heard about that, I assume?'

Frowning, Peter tried to piece together the fragments of the tale as told by others in the pub and wished he'd paid more attention at the time.

'Well, I got the gist of a tale, but not the details.'

Geoffrey sighed heavily as the curate regained his serious expression.

'Apparently, he breathed life into Oscar, that's the rabbit's name, by blowing into his mouth and whispering a magic word. Hilda is now convinced of his powers and runs around the place chanting some magic word.'

'And that's what you were talking to her about?'

'We can't have that, Peter. We just can't.'

'No, of course not. I'm not sure I know what you want me to say…or do. May I ask a silly question?'

'Ask away.'

'This magic word, do you know what it is?'

'Toe-ker-nom…I think, or something very much like it, please don't ask me to spell it. I think that's what she said.'

Peter rubbed his chin, hoping this simple action would somehow prevent a fit of giggling. He coughed once more and waited for Geoffrey to speak.

'Find out what it means, that's something you can do. Eyes and ears, they are our best weapons at times like this, believe me. You don't think I'm over-reacting, do you?'

'Of course not. It's perfectly natural, and appropriate, to be concerned. I'll see what I can uncover.'

'Thank you. I know you'll do your best…oh and give my best to Jane.'

CHAPTER ELEVEN

Jane shook her head, perhaps a little too vigorously, 'No thanks, not when I'm driving. Just water. Ice if you have it.'

Peter gulped down some shiraz, poured a little more into the Bolognese sauce, and opened the freezer compartment of the fridge.

'Indeed, I do…and a slice of lemon for Madame?'

'Perfect. The pasta smells good. Love the apron, by the way.'

'Thank you, a gift from one of the parishioners. Pasta is one of my specialities. Curry is the other one.'

'Oh, I love a good curry.'

He stopped seasoning the sauce, 'Oh…no…I didn't mean…I love pasta too.'

The shiraz was working, he reckoned, better not overdo it, just stay calm. Perched on a stool with her left shoe dangling from a toe, Jane seemed perfectly content, relaxed even. She was definitely wearing more makeup than usual, her pale blue dress showing off her lightly tanned arms. He was glad he wore his new polo shirt, even though the smell of cooking always seemed to cling to his clothes.

'I think it's ready. Just got to grab a couple of plates from the cupboard and we're all set.'

Jane hopped down from her stool, 'Have you seasoned it? C'mere, shift yourself.'

Peter fetched the plates, relieved slightly that she was sufficiently chilled to take control.

She kicked off her shoes, served up the pasta and set the tiny kitchen table while he poured some more wine into his glass.

'Is it ok? I might have been too heavy with the Worcester sauce.'

'It's fine. Well done. I popped in to check on Marcia by the way, before I came over here, she's settled, quiet but happy enough. I asked her about the old photograph in the frame, you know the one, it has a picture of a priest, yes? I thought it might be some relative. I only asked about it to get a bit of conversation going.'

'Right. What did she say?'

'An old friend, apparently.'

He wondered why she chose this precise moment to say all this. Her voice was a tad too calm, business-like, as though she was still at work. Had he lost his touch? Did he need to change the subject, get her into something completely different? For a while, their eyes didn't meet, and the conversation stalled completely while the first few mouthfuls of pasta were consumed.

'Where did you do your training, Jane?'

'Manchester, when I finished Uni at Liverpool.'

The chat turned to Manchester and was suddenly much easier; they swopped stories and laughed and smiled in all the right places. Then the meal was over.

'Peter, do you have somewhere I can plug my phone in? Battery's getting very low, sorry, I should have checked it before I came out.'

'Over there by the work top. Are you on call most of the time?'

'No, but I like to keep it charged up, force of habit. Tell me more about this place, Clamford I mean, the famous statue, fascinating stuff.'

He knew he was on safe ground here. The village was surprisingly fruitful, with tales of intrigue and mystery. Jane's eyes were perpetually on his now, dancing with curiosity at every twist in the story.

'Like I say, I never actually got to meet Harriet Wilberforce, she died just before I arrived here. But, she's so real to me now, everyone has something to say about her, quite a lady, and the statue…well, sort of speaks for itself, yeah?'

'Absolutely! Takes some nerve to have a statue made of yourself, stark naked, with a lover at your feet. And then to have it deliberately planted where everyone can see it, forever. No wonder there was such a kerfuffle.'

'Hah, the ladies of the W.I. were not amused, especially after they'd commissioned a special commemorative plaque.'

'Not the statue they were expecting.'

'You could say that. But there's no denying it brings in the visitors.'

'She knew what she was doing alright. Who's the lover? The guy wrapped around her feet?'

'Ah well. That's tricky. Seems she and one of the local farmers, Roy Sudron, had a thing going on, so most folk think it must be him but if you go close up to the statue, it's difficult to tell because his face is pushed up against Harriet's legs.'

'I can't believe that I haven't got round to seeing it yet, been too busy, wrapped up in my job.'

'Well, any time you want to visit, I'll be pleased to show you.'

'I'd like that.'

'Coffee?'

'Thanks. Then I must be going, and you'll have the church service in the morning. It's been a lovely evening.'

Jane uncurled herself from her chair and unplugged her phone from the socket by the worktop, 'No messages, thank goodness.'

Peter had his back to her. There was more to him than she'd expected. The beard was too straggly, but she could live with that at a push, or persuade him to try the designer stubble look. He carried himself well, for a priest. She couldn't think of a reason why a clergyman shouldn't carry his weight well but all the same…It was his laugh that got to her, the twinkly eyes and careless tossing back of the head.

They took their time over the coffee; the small talk was easy and comfortable.

'Right. I must go. Thank you again.'

'You're welcome, next time call a taxi so you don't have to drive…'

He winced, flushed. Finally, at the very last, had he dropped the ball?

'Sorry, I didn't mean to assume, I mean I hope, maybe, there's another time…with curry…and wine.'

He sucked in air through his teeth and hung his head. Jane gently kissed his forehead and turned on her heels.

'Don't be stupid, Peter, I'd love to see you again.'

He squeezed past her and grabbed the handle of the front door to hold it open, as gentlemen like to do. It squealed on its hinges as the cool night air rushes in.

'Mind the…'

Too late, her shoe caught on the threshold and she lurched forward, her arms flailing out into the darkness of the pavement. Her right palm hit the cold, hard surface with a slap, but she managed to twist herself sideways to cushion the worst of the fall.

'Oh Lord! Are you ok…Jane? I'm so sorry.'

Jane lay still for a second while the curate, horrified, stood rigid.

Someone was approaching, running, heavy steps, must be a man, Jane could just make out his outline, then the shape of his body, tall, angular, a strong arm at her elbow.

'There you go Miss, no rush, you just take your time, I've got you. Can you sit up? That's good. Take a breather.'

Jane started to brush away at her arms and feet, 'Thank you, you're every kind. I think I'll be ok. Nothing broken. Just feel such an idiot, I didn't see it. Just a trip. No harm done.'

Jacob's strong arms supported her easily as she got to her feet, the gentle hands still at her elbows.

He whispered, 'Take it easy now, that's it. You'll be fine…TOCONOM.'

'What's that? Sorry, still a bit dizzy.'

'Good night, Miss, take care.'

Peter ushered her back into the cottage, but she resisted.

'No, I'm fine, honestly. Not your fault, Peter, don't let it spoil our evening. I'll be fine…promise…goodnight.'

He watched her car pull away, then glanced down the row of cottages.

Jacob unlocked his front door, unaware of the curate's bitter stare of blazing resentment.

CHAPTER TWELVE

Jacob's shoulders rose, he inhaled deeply and placed his hands on his knees. The Sunday early evening air was cooling now, there may even be a damp dew first thing tomorrow but the sun would soon burn it off. He'd made a decent start, clearing away broken seed trays and worn-out gardening tools, finding hidden hooks on the sides of the shed walls to hang rakes and forks and the rest. Tomorrow, he'd make a start on the far corner where the workbench waited in the gloom.

The crusty red brick of the garden wall was warm to the touch, the air thick with insect humming but otherwise calm and serene. He trod slowly past Arthur the scarecrow. No sign of Snowy Elstrop, Trevor or Fred today, nor any of the regular volunteer gardeners.

There was a water hose attached to an outside tap, and it still worked. Stripped to the waist, Jacob let the cool water flow down from his head and shoulders to his jeans, until the sound of gravel crunching beneath the tyres of the familiar Land Rover became impossible to ignore and he forced himself to look up.

Camilla's voice travelled easily across the lawns. She was wearing a dress of some light pink material, her hair loose, and she was laughing. At her side was a man Jacob had yet to meet. He watched them as they walked together, absorbed in conversation, towards the main entrance to Brompton Hall.

Jacob lingered a few seconds more at the water tap before deciding to crossing the few yards to the edge of the lawn where he would surely be visible. Camilla was already inside the Hall entrance before the man spun around.

It was easy to guess what the man was saying and, sure enough, Camilla reappeared at the man's side. Now, they were waving at Jacob and coming over towards him.

'Well, hello.'

Her voice was light and crisp.

'Hello. I've just packed in for the day. Thought I'd make a start on the shed. You look as though you've been somewhere very nice.'

She gave a little chuckle of laughter.

'I could say the same about you…'

Jacob quickly pulled his tee shirt over his damp body, 'Sorry, I just…'

'No need to apologise. Must have been hot work today.'

The man looked away for a second, when he finally spoke there was a studied casualness about his voice, and a tension in his jaw, 'Surprised you weren't at the cricket. Big match with Larchester. Most of the village was there.'

'Oh, aye. That's good. I hope everyone enjoyed themselves. I heard them talking about it, but I thought I'd crack on here.'

Camilla ran her hand through her hair, 'It was lovely. Really exciting. This is Roy, by the way. Roy Sudron.'

'Pleased to meet you, Roy.'

Jacob dried his palms on his jeans and extended his hand.

'And you must be Jacob. Your ears must have been burning.'

'Oh…why's that, then?'

Camilla was giggling now. There was still a lingering tension deep in Roy's voice.

'Seems you've been giving Freddie Bairstow some coaching tips. He knocked up a good innings today. Everybody was chuffed for him, even the Larchester lads gave him a round of applause. He'll be getting free pints in the Fox and Grape for a while.'

'Good for him. It was nothing really, just needed a word of encouragement. He's a good lad, learns fast.'

They looked at him slightly oddly and silence fell on them. Camilla spoke first, 'Well, look, you deserve a beer yourself after your hard work. Roy, why don't you fetch a few cans, we can sit out here while it's still light, shame to waste this glorious weather.'

'Oh no, thank you, that's very kind, I don't want to intrude.'

'You're not.'

Roy stiffened, then sighed. He would not argue, 'Right then. Tell you what. Why don't you come with me, help me carry them out?'

'Are you sure, I'm scruffy like…'

'Nonsense, you go with Roy while I have a quick look at your handiwork in the shed. Fetch whatever you like, there's beer or lager. Mine's a shiraz, please.'

The polished wooden floor creaked under the weight of Jacob's heavy shoes as he followed Roy through the splendid oak doors at the entrance to Brompton Hall.

'You wouldn't make a burglar wearing those.'

Jacob forced a little laugh from somewhere as he removed them.

'There's a kitchen at the back of the house, are you a beer or a lager man, Jacob?'

'I'm not a big drinker to be honest. Whatever you have, thanks.'

The door to the large drawing room was slightly ajar, allowing a glimpse of part of a panelled wall, one or two watercolours, and the corner of one of the huge oak tables.

'Upstairs is private, ok? Down here, that room we passed is the drawing room, that's where business is done. What's she paying you, by the way? If you don't mind me asking.'

Jacob stopped in his tracks behind Roy who turned to face him.

'Look Roy. I think you must have got me wrong.'

'Have I?'

'I reckon. Why did you tell me upstairs is private? Did you think I was going to snoop around the place when nobody was looking?'

They stared at each other for a few seconds, but Roy couldn't hold his gaze very long.

'Why don't we start again, eh, Roy? You'll get no trouble from me, I'm here to do work, that's all. Now, why don't we fetch those drinks?'

'Fair enough.'

'And since you asked. We agreed on an arrangement…for the work.'

'Right. And Snowy Elstrop, is he giving you any grief?'

'Good as gold.'

Jacob gave a nod of finality and they headed for a narrow corridor, down a couple of steps to the darkness of the kitchen. Two dim ceiling lights flickered into life.

'Brompton isn't really as big as folk sometimes imagine, the whole place needs rewiring, God knows when it was last done, but it would be an expensive job in an old place like this, all high ceilings and panelled walls. It doesn't get much light in here, but it's so cool for storing food and drink.'

Roy grabbed a couple of cans from the large American-style fridge and retrieved a wine bottle from the rack.

'It's only a screw top but she won't mind, can you pass me that clean glass over there? You alright with drinking straight from the can? Means less to carry that's all.'

'Alright with me.'

Jacob detected a noticeable softening of tone in Roy's voice and on the way back to the garden, he allowed himself another quick glance through the open door of the drawing room.

'Impressive, isn't it? I bet you haven't seen a room like this, before, right?'

Jacob let the question float away, unanswered, and nudged the door open a little more with his shoeless feet. The décor remained as it has been, more or less, for generations. The watercolours had not faded in the sombre light restricted by the heavy velvet curtains, the huge stone fireplace still bore the same marks from the days when it was in constant use, the massive oak tables and sideboard still imbued the room with the reassuring smell of fine old wood polish.

'Beautiful.'

By the time they returned to the lawn, the light was fading fast. A tiny breeze stirred the tops of the trees and the humming of insects drifted over to where Camilla had set up a small glass-top table and three chairs, setting the tone with a beaming smile.

'The perfect ending to a lovely day.'

Jacob pressed a cold can of lager against his brow.

'You really have been hard at it while we've been sunning ourselves at the cricket. The shed's already looking much tidier.'

'Aye well, I'm used to hard work. If you like, I can start on the greenhouses and the far paths when I'm done with the shed. Won't take too long. It's a fine place. A lovely lady should have a lovely garden to walk in.'

The words hung between them in the evening air. At last, Roy spoke.

'My parents told me about you, about the other day. Mother gets tired with Dad in that wheelchair. We appreciate your kindness, my dad has his good and bad days but you made it a good day for him, and mother of course.'

Jacob could sense Camilla looking sideways at him, waiting for some kind of response, but Jacob offered none and pulled at the opener of his lager can. She turned her stare to the label on the wine bottle. It hadn't occurred to her she could actually be nervous in the presence of this man, but she was. As if reading her thoughts, Jacob took her glass and filled it half full with shiraz, then placed it slowly in front of her. Still, there was silence.

Roy rubbed the back of his neck and pretended to swat away a fly. Camilla thought she could almost hear him thinking a thousand things he chose not to say. It felt like Jacob was the host and they were the guests.

'They tell me you're staying at Marcia Bennett's old place. How long will you be staying around here? Not that we want you to go, good handymen are worth their weight in gold.'

Her voice was a little too urgent, but her question moved things along.

'Aye, that's right. Ted Smailes is renting it out to me for a while. Grand little place, spotless and it has everything you could want. My horse, Joey, is in his stable, at his farm. He's getting on, but he still has a few years left in him. Good people they are. Not sure how long it will be for, but we'll see. I like it here. I like to get to know folk. People are fine.'

'Well, they certainly seem to have taken to you.'

'Oh well, I say if a man can't do a good turn for his neighbour, then what's the world coming to?'

'You seem to live a pretty free sort of life, if you don't mind me saying.'

'I don't mind at all.'

Roy leaned forward, his eyes suddenly alive with curiosity, 'I've lived in Clamford all my life, apart from an agricultural college. It's where I belong. Don't you miss having roots to put down though, somewhere to belong? Sorry. Tell me if I'm poking my nose in. Just interested, that's all.'

'No need to be sorry, you've been very kind and I appreciate it. See, I have roots alright but I reckon my roots are in the land, all of it I mean. Listen to the insects just now and the birds earlier on. Beautiful. I love all that. I know how to live, don't you worry. I'm a contented man. Life's been good to me.'

Camilla nodded and rested her hand on Jacob's arm.

'And I bet you live each day like it was the last day of your life.'

'Aye, that's right.'

'You remind me of someone I met once.'

Jacob tossed his head back to finish off his lager and whispered to the sky.

'Toconom.'

CHAPTER THIRTEEN

Millers shop was open as usual today, of course. Business had been brisk, and the sisters seemed to have acquired a new energy. Joan baked some cakes over the weekend and was making sure they were clearly visible in the window. She was thinking of baking some loaves this week, like the ones they used to make years ago before they bought bread in from wholesalers. When the school closed for the Summer, they would be even busier than usual.

Cissie was about to boil the kettle to make tea when the bell above the door rang out again. It was the vicar's wife, Julia.

'Oh! I do love the gorgeous smells whenever I come in here.'

'I was just about to make tea, would you like a cup, dear?'

'How kind, thank you. I only came in for some biscuits, but those cakes in the window are tempting me, I'll take one for Geoff and the children, it'll cheer him up.'

'Oh dear, is he down in the dumps, then? He always seems so calm and assured, doesn't he, Joan?'

'Calm and assured, yes I agree, Ciss.'

Soon, the three women lost track of time. They had tea and biscuits, congratulated themselves on the splendid catering at Saturday's cricket match, chatted to a few regular customers who came and went, shared a few thoughts on the latest from the Women's Institute, and the tedious Summer Fair at

Larchester which often attracted the wrong sort of people so that the locals stayed away.

Finally, Julia checked her watch.

'Don't forget your cake, I hope the family enjoys it.'

Joan could see Julia's hesitancy and went to the window.

'It's on the house.'

'Oh no, I couldn't, let me pay.'

'Nonsense. If it'll cheer up your husband, well then…tell him we hope he feels better soon.'

'It's a bit of a fuss over nothing, really. Hilda's playing up and it's troubling him. Well, what I mean is, not playing up so much, she's a little treasure really, but coming out with things she's picked up. You know, the way children sometimes do.'

'We know exactly what you mean, don't we, Cissie?'

'We do, Joan, we do.'

Julia forced a smile and attempted a little diversion, 'What do you make of the chap who's living in Marcia's old cottage? I hear quite a lot about him, they say he's doing some work at Brompton Hall.'

'Yes he is, comes in every morning for a few things, such a lovely man.'

'My word, seems he can do no wrong.'

Silence.

Joan gave a curious glance towards her sister, 'He showed me some exercises to help with my aches and pains and, do you know, they worked a treat, didn't they Cissie?'

'Worked a treat, Joan.'

'Glad to hear it. A miracle cure!'

Joan shot another glance at Cissie. What was Julia's problem? It was not like her to be snide. Why the sudden scorn in her voice? Was it fear? Did she know something?

In a voice that was brittle, too loud with more than a hint of defiance, Joan made her position clear, 'Well, we take as we find, don't we Cissie? He seems a lovely, decent man and we like him.'

Julia seemed taken aback for a moment, 'Oh, I didn't mean to imply anything, I think you may have misunderstood, sorry.'

She broke off, a pained expression spreading over her face, her eyes focussed on somewhere far beyond the confines of the shop. Cissie stepped forward, her plump rosy cheeks more flushed than ever, her hands gently resting on Julia's, soft and strangely reassuring.

'Is there something troubling you, dear?'

'No, no, really. I'm being silly. It's just that one of the

children, Hilda, seems to have got it into her head that this Jacob fellow can perform real miracles, I mean real miracles. Geoffrey's concerned. We're probably overreacting. Like I say, it's all very silly.'

'Ah, we understand, don't we, Joan?'

'Of course, we do, Cissie. The things children come up with. I wouldn't worry too much. You should try to meet Jacob, he's ever such a friendly chap. Put your mind at rest.'

Julia's smile broadened.

'You're quite right, of course. One shouldn't try to make judgements of people one hasn't even met.'

'Here, don't forget your cake, and you take these chocolates for the children and share some with the vicar. Give him our love…and stop all that worrying nonsense. These things blow over.'

CHAPTER FOURTEEN

By mid-morning, the following day, the sun had failed to penetrate the thick layer of cloud that hung over the vale. It was warm and sticky, there were no shadows and no signs of rain. In the dark shed, the two weak light bulbs flickered defiantly but made little impression on the dim interior where Jacob had already put in a couple of hours toil. An old tarpaulin was laid out near the door, on which he placed a few pieces of broken fencing, some chipped bricks, tiles and smashed plant pots. The ancient workbench in the corner was, at last, clearly visible. Under it, there were several tools, a vice and a lathe. With a drop of oil and elbow grease, he reckoned they could be good as new, almost. That could wait 'till tomorrow. For the time being, he would clean the place up and make a start on the row of greenhouses. He would have a word with Snowy Elstrop to use his van to take the rubbish to the local skip.

He stepped out into the walled garden to clear his brain, sip some tea from his flask and grab a sandwich bought earlier at Millers shop. Looking around, there were a few volunteers working in the fruit and vegetable plots, but no sign of Trevor or Fred just yet.

The sound of a car coming up the drive brought him to attention. When it turned into the lawned grounds and halted at the front of the Hall, he didn't recognise it, nor the driver. Geoffrey Roper was alone and without his dog collar. It took several knocks and three attempts with the bell to convince him that no one was home at Brompton this morning. He was about to return to his Volvo when Jacob called over with a wave of his tired arms.

'They're not here, been gone since an hour ago. Can I help you, friend?'

The vicar, so often prone to stress headaches, pressed a hand to his brow while bouncing a little on his heels. He nodded a silent acknowledgement, his eyes trying to absorb any notable features of the man before him. Immediately, he observed that this chap was what they call strapping, probably over six feet, with shoulders and arms capable of carrying one of Len Hewitt's beer barrels without breaking sweat. Were it not for the greying hair, he could pass for a guy in his mid-thirties while the likelihood remained that he was older than the vicar. Despite this, Geoffrey suspected that time had not always been kind to him, yet he bore the countenance of a calm, almost cheerful figure. Was this Jacob, he wondered.

'My name's Jacob, what's yours?'

'Ah…er…Geoffrey Roper…Geoff, pleased to meet you, Jacob.'

He anticipated correctly that Jacob's handshake would be warm and strong.

'I don't know rightly when they'll be returning like, I just work here but I suppose I could leave them a message, if you like, if that will help.'

'Thank you, that's most kind. Actually, I have other errands on my list today, so I may call again this afternoon. It's Miss Wilberforce I was intending to speak to.'

Jacob remained silent.

'So, you're the new man around here. What sort of work are you doing?'

'Why don't you come and have a look? If you have time, that is. Seeing as how you've had a wasted journey an'all.'

Geoffrey allowed himself a smile. His headache was retreating rapidly, replaced by a satisfying feeling that his morning may not be unprofitable after all, if he could discover more about this fellow.

A couple of heads popped up from the vegetable rows as Geoffrey followed Jacob to the shed by the far wall. A man's voice rose above the sound of labour.

'Morning Vicar.'

Geoffrey smiled in the direction of the voice, a little disappointed that he could not remain undetected a while longer. When they arrived at the shed door, he whispered, 'Probably should have said. I'm in charge at St Barnabas's, here in Clamford.'

'Of course, you are. I have some tea left in my flask if you'd care for some.'

Not the response Geoffrey expected. Was this Jacob fellow too dim to be surprised?

'Oh, no thanks.'

Inside, the place smelled of paraffin and wood preserver, while the floorboards creaked under their feet but were freshly scrubbed and even. Two large bags had been stuffed with bits of paper, assorted chippings, dust, dead insects and the remains of spiders' webs wrapped in newspaper. The surface of the workbench in the far corner had been cleared of all tools except the lathe, and a heavy vice had been cleaned up, assembled and attached to the side. In the gloom of the two flickering light bulbs, they surveyed each other; Geoffrey's wariness began to ebb.

'I'm glad we've bumped into each other, Jacob. It's reassuring to put a face to a name.'

Jacob said nothing, fully aware of the virtues of patience and silence in these sorts of conversations.

'I've heard favourable things about you, I must say. And even my daughter was most impressed by your actions when the school rabbit was almost killed.'

The vicar watched for a reaction.

'I do what I can. Folk here have been great to me, very kind and hospitable. Children see stuff and they don't understand what it is they're seeing. Fact is, some grown-ups are no different to their kids. I know what you might think of me, maybe you keep them thoughts locked up, like the tools in this 'ere shed, sort of a secret but they're there all the same. No worries, I say. That's alright by me. Like I say, I just do what I can.'

'Yes. Commendable, indeed.'

'What else is a man supposed to do? You tell me, Geoff.'

The question coaxed a smile from the vicar. He ran his palm slowly, back and forth, across the surface of the workbench before speaking, 'You are not at all who I expected.'

Each surveyed the other again. Jacob held out his hand. Geoffrey accepted it.

A knock on the shed door caused them both to look up. One of the gardening volunteers leaned in, he ignored Jacob and stared intently into Geoffrey's face.

'Can I have a word, Reverend, before you go, about next week's church council? Couple of things have come up. No rush, just when you' can spare a second or two. Didn't expect to see you, so I thought…you know…while you're here.'

'Yes, yes. Of course, Frank. Be with you in a second.'

Geoffrey turned to Jacob, 'Perhaps we'll bump into each other again. Take care.'

'Toconom.'

Jacob nodded and touched his cap, then squeezed past to disappear into the greenhouse.

CHAPTER FIFTEEN

Geoffrey clasped the phone close to his chest and sighed, 'Oh, dear me. Thank you for letting me know, Peter. I was thinking I might pay a visit to Ramsden House this morning, so this has confirmed things for me, I'll let you know what's what. Bye.'

He'd been thinking about Jacob and reflecting on their conversation with more than a little satisfaction, but now there were other pressing matters to attend to. This was a day for the dog collar.

Julia was in the kitchen pouring cereal into bowls for Hilda and Aidan, 'Shhh…don't shout at your brother like that. Have you both washed your hands? Let me see…both sides…good. Where are your shoes, Aidan?'

The chatter didn't falter when Geoffrey walked in.

'Any coffee going?'

'Sit down, Geoff, if you're doing visits, you need something on your stomach, have some toast and marmalade.'

'Have to make it quick, then. Peter's just called. I need to pop over to Ramsden House.'

Julia waited for the children to settle down and loaded some bread slices into the toaster.

'Problem?'

'Well, yes. Marcia Bennett had a fall through the night and one of the other residents passed away earlier, a chap who used to come to St Barnabas's. There's a family member wants to have a word with me.'

'Oh, poor Marcia, how bad is it?'

'Not a lot of detail from Peter, I'll speak to Jane, of course.'

Julia poured coffee into two large mugs, suppressing a smile, 'How are those two getting on, has Peter said anything?'

Geoffrey shook his head emphatically.

'Hmmm, I wonder how the pasta meal went down.'

'None of our business, really.'

'Oh, come on! It's *me* you're talking to.'

'I expect you'll find out soon enough, my love, it's one of your many talents.'

She laughed delightedly and gripped his hand.

The Volvo took a little less than thirty minutes to arrive at the care home. Two residents, wheelchair bound, had been pushed out to the forecourt to enjoy some people watching, though there were few visitors this morning. Geoffrey offered a courteous nod and frowned as the familiar odours met his nostrils. He signs the visitors' book and examined the last few entries, squeezed the antiseptic dispenser and made for the corridor leading to Jane Simpson's office. He could hear some music coming from the resident's lounge but, otherwise, it was quiet.

'They've kept Marcia in at King George's as a precaution, but they've just informed me it's bad bruising, nothing broken, and they're hoping to release her later today or tomorrow morning.'

'How did it happen?'

'Come along to her room, I can show you better in there.'

They passed along another corridor where a notice board displayed a small poster.

FRIDAY MORNING

GEMMA FROST

CHIROPODIST EVERY FRIDAY AT TEN

FOLLOWED BY SONGS FROM THE SHOWS

COFFEE MORNING WITH JANEY JONES

ALL WELCOME

Marcia's room was at the end of the corridor, with a clear view of the entrance and car park. To the best of his recollection from previous visits, it all looked undisturbed, 'Ah, that's nice. Lily of the Valley, takes me back, my dear mother used it all the time.'

'She asked one of the staff to open the window a little for some fresh air. Minutes later, there was a bit of a commotion. It seems she was sitting in her favourite place, by the window in her armchair. The hospital told me she'd suffered a bee sting so…we assume that Marcia was, maybe, standing up to swot it away when she lost her balance. The armchair may have helped to cushion her fall. Who knows? We'll be able to investigate properly when she's back. The staff assure me that all correct procedures were adhered to.'

'I'm sure that's right. Old people have falls.'

'The good news is that she seems fine other than bruising and shock, no doubt. She may be a modest, private sort of lady, but she's a resilient woman is our Marcia, a fighter. So…nothing broken thank goodness, apart from this.'

She turned to the coffee table, picked up the old framed photograph of the priest, and gingerly handed it to Geoffrey. The glass was cracked in two and there was damage to one of its corners, 'You just watch, she'll be more upset about this than anything else that's happened. I shall have to look into getting it fixed.'

Geoffrey's face was a picture of concentration, 'May I take this, Jane? I have a feeling I know just the chap who will mend this. Please tell Marcia that I promise to take good care of it.'

'Well, if you're sure, yes, that would be excellent.'

'Good, well, I have to see someone else while I'm here, as you know, but thanks for your time. Is there anything else we need to talk about? I expect Peter will come by at some point, so if there's anything you feel…'

'No, I don't think so.'

CHAPTER SIXTEEN

Fred Pickles was seventy-eight. The years have flown quickly since Cecil Rowntree, co-founder of a family accountancy firm in Larchester, hosted a small retirement reception in Fred's honour, at the Fox and Grape. With Evelyn at his side, Fred enjoyed the spotlight that night when life had rarely felt better. There were no children, she could not conceive, but the Good Lord provided immunity from all major crises and the Pickles took great comfort from this blessing. Then the world stopped. Cancer took Evelyn ten years ago and, though he would never admit this to anyone, not even Tattoo Trevor, there had not been a week when he hadn't longed for death. Yet, here he was, in this lovely place he knew so well, among the plants and trees at Brampton, watering can in hand, examining the vine on the far wall to see how much it had grown this week. If he'd been a wiser man, he told himself, perhaps he'd have discovered new hobbies and interests to fill the days. He should learn to say no when folk asked him to look over their accounts. At home, he had a cupboard full of unopened bottles of wine, port and whiskey from the grateful inept.

This was what Fred Pickles did best: putting on a brave face, tending to the garden, chatting occasionally to the other Brampton volunteers, listening to Tattoo Trevor's tales and sharing his tea and sandwiches.

Nothing ever changed much, yet Fred couldn't figure out what made this week feel a little different. Somehow, the clay seemed less heavy to the touch; the air was lighter and sweet on the tongue, the colours of the garden richer somehow. He felt a little ashamed that he hadn't noticed, before now, how glorious the old sycamore was at this time of year…until Jacob pointed it out this morning. And the other day, he couldn't help himself. He'd hidden behind its trunk, crouched down, and rubbed his palms along its bark, listening to the clattering of rubbish being chucked from the old shed, and repeating that funny word that Jacob uses… Toconom.

It was a good feeling, and today this was all he needed to get him through.

The long greenhouse was looking much better. Fred remembered once taking the job on himself: to climb up stepladders to polish up the glass then strip down the wooden racking, sort out the decent pots and containers from the rubbish. That was likely ten years ago, he wouldn't like to take it on today. His fingers worked well enough and his legs haven't let him down yet, but he couldn't lift heavy weights these days and his limbs took longer to recover from a morning's work.

Evelyn enjoyed dancing; they both did, but she was extra keen. Swimming was his thing, every Saturday.

He dreaded the prospect of dependency.

'How do Fred, fancy a cuppa?'

Jacob's call startled him and, for a second or two, he was a little disorientated. There was no sign of Tattoo Trevor's bike, and Snowy Elstrop and the others were over in the far vegetable plot. Slowly, he straightened and shuffled past some lavender bushes towards the shed.

'Well, I never thought I'd see this old shed looking so good, it's only ever been used as a dumping ground since I don't know when.'

Jacob had rigged up a couple of planks and two sturdy crates to make a bench seat, 'Sit yourself down, my friend. I reckon we've both earned a break, eh?'

He filled two mugs from his flask and handed one to Fred, watching the old man's hooded eyes, slightly sunken yet alert, observing the loose skin of his arms and the age spots on the backs of his hands. As they absorbed the quiet warmth of the shed, words seemed unnecessary until Fred's gaze rested on the renovated workbench.

'Will you look at that? Amazing. I'd forgotten that was in here, you know. '

Jacob's voice dropped to a whisper, 'Sheer neglect, that's the truth of it. Just a bit of care, and some elbow grease, and she scrubbed up good as new, well…almost.'

'Aye. We all need a bit of that, some of us more than others!'

The old man's eyes crinkled in delight at his own joke.

'You do well for your age, Fred. Don't be so hard on yourself.'

'I do my best.'

'I know that.'

'I try to stay positive. Coming here to Brampton, close to nature like, makes the days go by easier, seeing things growing, helping them along. But getting old is no picnic.'

'Yeah, I hear what you say. Can I ask you something? You scared of it, growing old, I mean?'

'We all are, aren't we? It comes to us all. Those times when you realise you can't be climbing up ladders any more to paint windows or fix tiles. Or, you can't tot up a row of figures as fast as you used to. You start to think about things more, instead of doing things, know what I mean? Before you know it, you start to have regrets you never knew you had 'till now.'

Jacob smiled and laid a hand on Fred's shoulder, 'No need for regrets. What's past is past and done, eh? Do yer best, that's all, learn as yer goes along. Tell you what I reckon. I reckon when we're young, we're too busy to think, too busy and wrapped up in doing this and that with no time to sit back and think. I heard someone say once, if I can remember right…if you can learn how to grow old properly, and how to die proper, you'll learn how to live proper. Good, that, isn't it? Good words, eh? Thinking stuff up like that, good that is. Good.'

'Aye lad. This 'ere garden is a good place to think.'

'The better for having folk like you to tend to it, Fred.'

They slid into half a minute of silence.

'What's that you got there on the bench?'

'Oh, that, it's summat I'm working on. Just a little job. An old photo frame, it got a bit damaged, so he asked if I can fix it.'

'You mean Roy Sudron?'

'No, not Roy, the vicar, Geoff.'

'Oh. The Reverend Roper. So that's it. I saw him coming and going. Can I have a look?'

'Careful mind, the glass is broken. In fact, while you're here, I may as well take it apart. Can't have you cutting yourself.'

'Aye lad, I don't care for the sight of blood, 'specially my own.'

Their laughter was easy and unforced, flowing gently between them as Jacob helped Fred to raise himself up from the makeshift seat. The old man stood at his shoulder as the damaged frame was carefully dismantled and the little retaining clips were slid away to release the pieces of shattered glass.

'I wonder who the old priest is in the picture.'

'Dunno. It belongs to the old lady who used to live in the cottage where I'm staying. Geoff was telling me. She had a fall recent like, an accident, and this was broken.'

'Oh dear, Miss Bennett. Lovely lady, used to teach at the village school. I hope she's alright, she's well thought of in these parts.' Jacob placed the photograph to one side and examined the frame, 'Should be easy enough.' 'I might have some glass at home. I can fetch it if you like. Might fit that frame, otherwise, you'll need a glass cutter.'

Jacob nodded in agreement and pointed to the plastic crate beneath the workbench.

'There's a cutter in there, hardly been used.' Fred edged closer, 'What's that? Under the photograph.'

When Jacob picked up the old picture, a smaller photograph, almost half the size, dropped to the bench, 'Look you here. I wonder why she kept two in the same frame. Probably a mistake, it got stuck to the back of the other one and stayed there, forgotten about.'

Fred examined the smaller, slightly blurred image of a young man, could be in his late teens, wearing a merchant navy uniform. The smile was open and friendly. This was a man pictured among friends, young and happy. There was nothing written on the reverse, other than letters B and S.

'Ours not to reason, Jacob.'

'Aye. I'll point it out to Geoffrey; he can decide what's to be done with it.'

CHAPTER SEVENTEEN

Snowy Elstrop's eyes were on stalks, Sandra Hewitt was wearing scarlet tonight. Propping up the bar in the Fox and Grape, she was having a night off while Len looked after everything with a local youth brought in for cover over the summer months. It was a lace outfit, cut to expose acres of thigh and supported, just, by spaghetti shoulder straps. As she reached across Snowy to spark up her lighter, her eyes remained fixed on the mirror behind the bar till, through which she could see every customer who entered.

The pub was half empty, Len would say it's half full, real drinking time would start later.

'Well, talk of the devil.'

Snowy directed his attention away from Sandra's cleavage to the door through which Peter Stephenson strode, mechanically and silently, hands in pockets, rugby shirt flapping over his jeans.

Len required no prompting and Peter's pint was pulled before the Smailes brothers had thought of something funny to say. This was just the sort of scene that fired Snowy's fertile imagination into overdrive, the sort that stirred up in him a profound and irresistible pleasure. Eyes dancing with mischief, he waited for the curate to gulp down most of his drink and order a second, before taking up his theme.

'Steady on lad, it's early yet.'

Peter stiffened visibly, 'I'm fine.'

'You want to tell yer face that.'

'Leave it, Snowy. Not in the mood. '

A pinging noise resounded from the back pocket of the curate's jeans, he reached down for his mobile phone, glanced at a text message and replaced it.

'Aww. Tell yer uncle Snowy all about it…'

The vicious glare from the curate was unexpected and shocking. Sandra knew enough about men to understand that it was also dangerous, 'You heard him…leave it.'

She nodded at the dartboard, and it took a full ten seconds before Snowy dutifully retreated to the company of a few regulars sitting in the corner.

'Thanks Sandra, sorry about that. I'll go over and pacify him soon. Just need a few minutes to think, know what I mean?'

'You go right ahead luv, and do your thinking…anything I can do? To help, I mean, I'm a good listener, goes with the job.'

'To tell the truth, I wouldn't know where to start.'

'Can't be as bad as that, can it?'

'That's just it. I have no reason to feel sorry for myself. No one has died. I love my job, I love it here. There's no bad news really, it's just that…I don't know who I am anymore.

'Sounds stupid I know. A few days ago, I could describe exactly who I thought I was.'

Sandra exhaled deeply, a cloud of vapour from her e-cigarette enveloped them both, 'Well luv, something must have set you off. Is it a woman, by any chance?'

Peter knew that she knew. She must have heard from somewhere. The word was out. For a moment, he wanted to tell her to get lost, but there was no escaping this need to release the poison that had found its way into his system, creating such a horrible burden of anger and bitterness. Geoffrey couldn't help, not this time, nor could Julia, they're too close. Sandra, on the other hand...

'It seems I may well have cocked things up with a lady I've grown very fond of...'

'Aha.'

And so, Peter related the story of Saturday evening's pasta supper with Jane.

'Everything had gone so well but, when she tripped over like that I was rooted to the spot, mortified, standing there like a complete prat, then this fellow Jacob appears from nowhere and does precisely what I should have been doing.'

'And that's it?'

'That's it, all over.'

'You sure, I mean, have you spoken to her, whoever she is?'

Peter shook his head and signalled to Len for another beer.

Sandra snorted in derision, 'Well, beer's not going to help. Let me ask you something…do you fancy me?'

Peter's jaw gaped open. The urge to walk away returned. Instead, he stared into her mascara-painted eyes, astonished and bewildered.

'Well, I mean to say, Sandra, I find you…what shall I say?'

'Say it.'

'I find you very…friendly and…'

Her grin turned to laughter, 'Men are such bloody stupid idiots. Alright, another question: do you trust me?'

'Yes, of course. I think. Yes.'

'Then listen to what I'm saying. Ok ? Grow up, for God's sake! You think she doesn't want to know you any more, eh? Let me tell you something. She's wondering why you haven't called her. You prat. She already knows you're a bit of a joke, all men are, but that's something us women have to live with. She doesn't mind that. She knew it when she accepted a date. What angers her is that you think you already know her and so you assume you know what she thinks…about you and about Jacob. Nothing annoys a woman more than that. But, the truth is you know nothing. So, stop fretting like a daft kid, get on the phone and call her. What have you got to lose? She knows you were mortified when she tripped, believe me. If you weren't, then that would have been a lot worse and we wouldn't be having this chat 'cos you'd already be dead meat in her eyes. And don't go thinking it's all Jacob's fault for stepping in like he did. He just did the right thing, that's all.'

'Wow! That's me told.'

'I've known a lot of men. When I met my Len, I found someone I could depend on. He understands me and I understand him…with all his faults, and Lord knows he's got plenty of those. That's how these things work. You need to find what works for you. If she's the right one, and you play your cards right instead of acting like a proper dope, then you'll look back on this and have a right old belly laugh…like I just did! Oh, and maybe you could say thanks to Jacob while you're at it.'

The curate took a swig of beer and composed himself, 'You're quite right, of course. I think I'll knock on his door in the morning.'

'No need to wait that long, he's just walked through the door.'

Peter swivelled on his heels. Before Jacob reaches the bar, a raised arm beckons to him, 'Hi there, I'm Peter. We haven't been introduced, but I just wanted to say…er…well…'

Sandra leaned forward, the scarlet material of her dress struggling to contain her breasts, 'What he's trying to say is thanks…and the pint there is for you.'

Jacob nodded, and they shook hands. Snowy was quick to seize the opportunity to regain some lost ground and was soon at Sandra's side. She nodded at her husband who knew exactly what to do.

'On the house, Snowy.'

'Ta very much and good health to one an' all.'

Jacob winked at Sandra and raised his glass, Toconom.'

CHAPTER EIGHTEEN

Tattoo Trevor's bike was propped up against the old shed. Inside, he sat on the makeshift seat with Fred at his side, while Jacob held up a rectangle of glass to the light.

'I don't know how you did it so quick, that frame's looking as good as new, Jacob, I reckon she'll not notice the difference, if you ask me.'

'Thanks Fred. I'm going to put it all back together, this afternoon, and then I'll give it back to Geoff and he can take it back to Miss Bennett. Job done.'

'What about the two photographs, are you going to put them back the way they were?'

'Yeah, strange that, isn't it? Could she have put it there deliberately or not? Who knows? Anyway, I was thinking of letting Geoff see for himself. He knows Miss Bennett so he may know what to do.'

Tattoo Trevor was on his feet, 'I need to get back on my bike, there's plenty needs doing on the allotment. See you later…just let's have another look at that picture before I go, eh?'

He took the little photograph outside where the sun was high in the sky and one or two volunteer gardeners were taking a break under the sycamore. Holding it in the palm of his large right hand, it seemed even more fragile and faded. Frowning, he studied the smiling sailor once more. It was not a boy's face that returned his gaze, neither did it belong to a fully mature man. It was an open face that had known joy and happiness but understood fear. A face he admired.

He waited a little longer before stepping back into the shed, 'I dunno what it is about this 'ere chap, but there's summat.'

Jacob had his back to him, but Fred seemed interested.

'What do you mean?'

'Dunno, Fred. Just summat. Can't put my finger on it. It's an old photo so I haven't a clue who it is but there's something about im. Anyhow, I'm off.'

No sooner had he disappeared than Snowy Elstrop appeared at the shed door, 'Now then lads, stand by your beds. Snowy's here!'

'Snowy, how are you doing this fine day?'

'Oh, I'm alright lad. The missus is not so bright. Got a bit of a strop on. Women eh? Anyhow, what you up to, Jacob? I hear you've got a few little jobs on the go. What you got there?'

'This? It's just a little job I'm doing for Geoffrey Roper, the vicar. Fixing up this old picture frame for Miss Bennett.'

'Miss Bennett, eh? Canny old stick, bit on the snooty side but nice woman for all that. Old photographs, dunno why folk hang on to them.'

Snowy stepped inside to inspect Jacob's handiwork, 'Well, can't stop gabbing 'ere all day, work to do. Be good boys, and if yer can't be good be careful.'

When Snowy's cackling faded into the distance, Fred and Jacob were silent for a while, their growing friendship no longer requiring the prop of constant conversation. A new sort of contentment had entered Fred's life, and he was grateful for it. He opened his little haversack and removed his lunch sandwiches.

'Cheese and pickle, want one?'

'My favourite. Thanks Fred.'

'My Evelyn used to make a good sandwich, she could think of all different things to put in them. Good cook was Evelyn.'

'Aye, that's good. How long were you married?'

Despite himself, Fred smiled with pleasure, 'Not long enough.'

'You must miss her.'

'Oh yes. Can I tell you something, Jacob?'

The question did not require a response, 'I nearly scared myself to death, just yesterday. I got up to come here. Had a shower, made my breakfast and something came over me. It made me feel scared and dizzy.'

'Yeah? You mean like a faint?'

'Not exactly, no. I had to sit down, though. It was strange. You see, I couldn't picture Evelyn's face. Can you believe that? I couldn't picture it: her eyes and nose or the shape of her mouth. It scared me and I felt ashamed.'

'No shame in that.'

'Well, it shook me, I can tell you. After a while, I made up my packed lunch and got ready to come here and…there she was again, clear as day in my head. And she was smiling the way she always used to. Better than before. Made me feel good, you know what I mean?'

'Aye. Maybe it's not such a bad thing. Sometimes a man needs to step away from stuff so he can see everything better, that's all. Like standing next to that big wall out there in the garden. If you stand there with your nose pressed up against the bricks, well, you're not going to see it proper. You need to step away from it, over the other side of the garden, then you'll see it.'

They ate in silence.

The air was a little cooler when Fred returned to the vegetable plots. He lingered for a while to dig over some weeds, had a few words with a lady volunteer from the village, then moved on to the small orchard, running his hand over the smooth bark of a plum tree. Jacob watched from the greenhouse and smiled when the old man removed his cap and wiped his brow with a handkerchief.

The afternoon rolled on until Jacob was left alone in the garden. It was less than a fortnight since he arrived in Clamford. In a few minutes, he would lock the shed and return to his temporary home in Marcia Bennett's old cottage and mull things over. He liked Clamford. Here at Brompton Hall, his work was almost complete. His old horse Joey was like a new beast, well fed having regained much of his strength at the Smailes's farm.

Jacob paused by the vine on the old brick wall to remove his shirt, just long enough to hear children yelling and laughing somewhere in the distance. Then it was quiet again except for the bees around the honeysuckle. He patted his hard stomach, remembering how pleasant it was to feel the cool, still air against his flesh. The sensation was reassuring. His mouth was open when he saw her, she was a few feet away, looking at him. There was no breeze to disturb her hair, she stood perfectly erect, feet together, hands clasped in front of her, eyes clear and steady, mouth ready to speak.

'I wondered if you would still be here. How are things going? My word, I must say you've done a good job, Jacob.'

He waited, 'Just cooling off, I didn't hear you coming. Been in the shed.'

Camilla tilted her head and stepped a pace towards him, the way he noticed her do that the other evening. Suddenly, there was a man's voice behind her, she spun round.

Geoffrey had his phone to his ear, his voice was too loud for such a still afternoon, 'Hilda! Please hand the phone back to Mummy, there's a good girl, yes, yes, …yes…please…hello?...hello?'

Geoffrey sighed, the day had been an unsatisfactory one, so far. His shoulders heavy with lassitude, he stared at the phone for a full minute, but it remained silent. Finally, he lifted his head and, like a magic trick, the garden began to weave its spell. Perhaps, he thought, this lovely place would set things right.

'Ah, good day to you all. I was passing and thought I'd just call by to see if, Jacob, you have, perhaps, managed to make a start on Marcia Bennett's photograph frame?'

Camilla's hands were placed firmly on her hips, 'What's this? Commandeering my workforce now, Vicar? Whatever next?'

If there was one thing Geoffrey disliked above all others, it was being teased; he suffered it as a child and now he felt the familiar taste of bile rising in his throat.

Jacob strode across to him with big solid steps, his hand outstretched in greeting, 'Good to see you again. I reckon Miss Bennett will be happy with it, come and have a look, see what you think.'

Camilla's eyes flicked between Geoffrey and Jacob, but she couldn't think of anything clever to say.

'Lead on, Jacob. You coming too, Camilla?'

Geoffrey noticed some tomato plants in pots that Jacob had placed by the tiny shed window, their delightful earthy smell filled the place. He felt better already.

'I need to transfer them toms to the greenhouse. Meant to do it earlier, but I got waylaid.'

Camilla shifted her weight from one foot to the other before stepping into the shed. Once in the shade, she stood with her head slightly bowed, feet together, like a child in fear of a lecture.

Jacob's voice was low and soft again as his big hands gingerly passed the photograph frame to Geoffrey, 'If you switch on the light there, you'll see better.'

'Nice work. Splendid. I'm sure she'll be delighted to have it back.'

Geoffrey passed it gently to Camilla, who gave the briefest of smiles, 'Who is this old priest in the picture, do you know?'

'I suppose I could find out but, when Peter asked her about him, she just said he was a good friend. One mustn't pry too closely, I find.'

'Hmmm, he looks a little stern, don't you think?'

'Well. I suppose so.'

Jacob turned to the workbench and carefully took a corner of the smaller photograph until he could lift it into his open palm, 'This chap looks happier, doesn't he? See here? This was squashed up behind the other one in the frame. What do you reckon, Geoff? Should I just pop it back in how it was, or what?'

Geoffrey scooped up the little picture of the merchant seaman and cupped it in both hands as if it was a tiny bird, 'It's probably been there years, long forgotten I should imagine.'

But his words sounded hollow. Jacob watched him closely, as if checking for any sign of recognition in the vicar's eyes. There was none.

'May I see?'

Camilla took her turn, holding the photograph up against the flickering light bulb. She turned it over again, this way and that, 'There's something written on the back.'

Her voice was milder now, suddenly interested, more confident for discovering something the two men seemed to have overlooked, 'It's just the letter B and S. Nothing else. Wonder what it means.'

Geoffrey took back the picture for a closer inspection, his lips pursed in concentration, 'I think I will show this to Miss Bennett. Yes, I think that's the thing to do. It could be nothing of significance, of course, but I believe it's the right thing to do.'

'Let me have another look…please.'

Camilla stared again at the smiling sailor, 'How strange…'

Her face faltered for a second, then she turned to Jacob with eyes wide and vulnerable like a young girl. He was still shirtless, his skin ruddy from the summer sun, the muscles in his arm taught as he leaned against the workbench. She turned her face away, back to Geoffrey's, 'I can't rid myself of the feeling that…I don't know…there's something familiar about him. Silly, I know, but…here, you take these things back to Miss Bennett. Give her my best regards.'

With that, she was gone.

Geoffrey stepped out of the shed and took a deep breath, 'Well thank you, Jacob, a marvellous job you've done. She'll be delighted. Bye for now.'

Jacob watched him go and stretched his arms to the sky before tracing his steps back to the garden wall to retrieve his shirt hanging from the vine.

'Toconom.'

CHAPTER NINETEEN

There was no need for Ted to duck to avoid the low beams at the entrance to the main passage in the Sudron's farmhouse, but he did. Doris, on the other hand, was a big woman with big hair that skimmed the oak wood. The living room door still creaked, she noticed, and Jim's little radio was tuned to Radio 4, of which she approved. Little had changed since she and Ted were last here, over two years ago, apart from the obvious. The painting with shire horses, the brasses, family photographs, the pottery on the delft rack, the copper scuttle, the vases of dried flowers, all lined up in the way she remembered them, nip clean and polished by Peggy's yellow duster. The ancient metronome on the old upright piano still looked as though it had never been used for many years.

It was in the centre of the room where they'd made the changes. Doris always admired Peggy's sofas, mainly because the Smailes's own living room wasn't big enough to house two such large pieces. Now, the sofas faced each other at the edges of a space where the two oak tables dominated everything else.

Jim looked bright in his wheelchair with his box of tissues, his newspaper, his glass of water, his magazines and radio.

'Well, this is nice, how are you feeling today, lad?'

Confidence came naturally to Doris, as she sat herself down nearest to the wheelchair and beckoned her husband to perch himself next to her by patting the sofa cushion, three times.

'Not so bad, Doris, thank you. Not so bad.'

Good, his voice was quite strong, she thought, 'Are the lads doing alright with everything?'

Jim raised his thumb and smiled, then Peggy appeared at the door, and Doris observed that she had removed her apron and had run a brush through her hair.

'That's better, it's hectic today. I left a joint in the oven for tonight as a treat and I had to check on it. Well, this is nice isn't it, Jim? Can I get you both a drink?'

Doris nodded approvingly, 'Do you know, I could just do with one of your gin and tonics, Peg. I was just saying to Ted how much we used to look forward to our whist nights and the gin and tonics, before Jim...'

Peggy laughed, 'If I'd known you were coming, I'd have asked our Colin to get some beers in for Ted. There might be a couple of cans out back, or we've got whisky, or brandy, whatever.'

'Ted's cut back a lot since, you know. Haven't you Ted?'

'Aye. I can speak for myself. I'll have a can of beer thanks Peggy. Failing that, I'll have a gin and tonic, ta very much.'

Peggy nodded and retreated to the kitchen.

Ted leaned in towards Jim, 'Well, my old pal, you're looking good. Still doing all your exercises?'

'She keeps me at it. I'm alright with me frame, I can get round the yard of a morning and, if I'm feeling up for it, I can manage for a bit with two sticks, but I soon get tired. I have a good family around me. I get spoiled. They push me around in this thing to get plenty of fresh air. In the evenings, I like to sit where you're sitting, Doris. Mind you, it's hard…not the same, but you've just got to get on with it, haven't you? No use moping about it.'

Doris patted the side of the wheelchair, 'And you're talking much better. You've done wonderfully well, all things considered.'

Silence.

'You know me, never was much of a talker, Peggy always says that. But thanks.'

Ted looked at Doris, almost mockingly, 'Not like some I could mention.'

They laughed, and the room seemed to brighten. Jim shifted in his wheelchair and turned to Ted, 'So, 'nuff about me. How are things going with you then, Ted? You've lost a bit more weight, I reckon. How's the old ticker? I hear tell you've got someone in Miss Bennett's place. Good chap, so they tell me.'

'Oh, I'm fine, lad. Got to keep going, eh? The boys take care of the farm, like your lads do here. Jacob's doing bits and pieces. That's the chap you mean. He's working up at the Hall at the minute. Good worker. You should get your Roy to take you into the pub of an evening, you could meet him. You'd like Jacob, he's a good fellow.'

Jim raised his thumb once more, 'Working up at Brompton Hall, you say? She never said 'owt about that. Must be doing alright if he got took on up there.'

'Oh, aye. Not sure how it came about, to be honest. It could be that your Roy set him on. That'll be the story. Doubt if Camilla would have 'owt to do with it.'

Doris placed her hands in her lap and sat up straight, 'Didn't Roy mention it? We thought you'd know. He's the talk of Clamford, this Jacob is. I wasn't happy at first, I can tell you but, fair enough, its all been good. He keeps his horse in our barn as well.'

Ted chuckled away to himself then opened up, 'Eh, Jim, I must tell you this, you'll never guess who I bumped into the other day, down by the river. Stepped out of a Land Rover, just like that, out of the blue, he…'

Peggy was back with the drinks, 'Here we are then, just like old times this isn't it?'

Doris laughed her throaty laugh, and Peggy settled into her seat, 'What was that you were telling Jim, Ted?'

'Oh no matter, it'll keep.'

Doris coughed a little too loudly, 'Tell them about Jacob, go on.'

'Aye, well, the first time I set eyes on the pair of them, Jacob and his old piebald, I thought to myself, what have we got here? Up by the statue it was. He said his horse was called Joey. What a state it was in. Looked about ready for Freddie Bairstow's yard.'

Doris chipped in, her eyes dancing with delight at the telling of the tale, 'Well, the horse is looking a ton better now, feeding on our bloody hay!'

'Language, Doris!'

'You're right, this is just like old times. You still know how to make a good gin and tonic, cheers!'

They settled into easy conversation as Peggy studied her guests. Doris would never change, her pink complexion glowing under that mop of silver grey, laughing at everything and anything but always with a watchful eye on the latest "doings" of Clamford, just in case she missed something. It was Ted who'd altered: less boisterous and noisy, slower these days on his feet, even his face was thinner and less bright as if he was not really taking in anything folk were saying, just putting a smile on to show everybody he still knew how to enjoy himself. Yet, he seemed to come alive whenever the talk turned to this Jacob fellow. Yes, it was the same old Ted but, in some strange way, Peggy didn't recognise him.

'Right then, why don't you stay for supper?'

'Oh, are you sure now? We don't want to cause more work for you.'

'Nonsense. Stay. It's a big joint, the boys won't mind a bit.'

Saying this out loud made it seem real.

And so the afternoon drifted into early evening, Doris sat with another drink in Peggy's kitchen as the meal was prepared, while Ted and Jim shared memories of happier times.

'He misses Tan, of course, Doris. We did think about getting another dog, but I told the boys we should wait a good bit longer. Soon though, I reckon, we'll get a pup.'

'He's doing very well is Jim. Men, eh? Can't be doing with them, can't do without them.'

'That's what they say about us.'

'How much gin do you put in these drinks, Peg, I'm already three sheets to the wind? Dunno how we're going to walk home.'

'One of the boys will run you and Ted back. Have another one, go on, the meat's nearly done.'

The women shared more laughter until the kitchen door burst open.

'Take your boots off, Colin, Ted and Doris are stopping.'

'Is Ted in the front room with Dad?'

'He is son, you look flushed, summat up, lad?'

'Come and look at this outside.'

Ted dashed in, his phone at his ear.

'No! Get away with you! Are you sure? Righto lad… you stay there… We'll see you later on…Bye.'

They rushed out into the yard where the air had cooled, and the sky was darkening, 'Over here! You can see from here!' They congregated by the large barn to watch a rising cloud in the sky coming from the direction of Brompton Hall. The still air was punctured by the sound of fire engines.

CHAPTER TWENTY

A small group of onlookers gathered near the entrance to Brompton Hall including Doris, Cynthia Pearson, wife of Maurice, Chair of the Parish Council, and Audrey Waterhouse with a couple of W.I. members. Their husbands stood a little further along the avenue of trees.

'It'll be youngsters, you can depend on it. I saw a couple of shifty characters near the cricket pavilion the other day.'

Doris was not convinced by Cynthia's confident prediction, but remained silent for the time being until Ted provided an update.

'And did you see who drove past? That lassie with the purple hair.'

'She did the radio stuff when Harriet's statue was unveiled. Looks like she's gone up in the world, she's doing the telly these days.'

'Fancy…you'd have thought she'd do something with her hair.'

It was mid-morning and the Fire Brigade had completed damping down. Purple girl was holding a microphone towards a police sergeant.

'At 2.50 this morning, we received reports of a fire at Brompton Hall gardens, a well-known landmark. It was well alight by the time the fire appliances arrived. No one was injured. It has caused a great deal of damage to the shed and its contents, estimated to run into several thousand pounds. Brompton Hall is, of course, a listed property. Because of the fire's proximity to trees and foliage and to the old Hall itself, there was some spreading of heat and flame to part of the building. It is fortunate it didn't spread further and cause even more destruction. In the event, although there is smoke damage to part of the Hall there is no structural damage. At the moment, we are treating the fire as suspicious. Enquiries into the incident are ongoing and we are appealing to anyone with information or saw any suspicious activity in the area to please come forward. There are far too many of these sorts of incidents in our region. They cause a great deal of harm and we are determined to get on top of this problem.'

Purple girl turned to Camilla who lowered her face towards the microphone, 'This is a punch in the guts, of course, these gardens are much loved and I am always grateful to the many volunteers who come every day to help look after the place. I am just so thankful that no one was hurt and the main building is relatively undamaged. We will put this right and carry on.'

Purple girl faced the camera, 'The village of Clamford is, of course, no stranger to publicity. Two years ago, the now famous…some would say infamous… statue of the late owner, Miss Harriet Wilberforce, was unveiled to public view and caused considerable controversy. Some called "the naked lady" an outrage, but it remains in place and attracts many visitors, each year, to this quiet corner of the north.'

The pungent remains of the shed lay in a smoking heap. A steel frame chair, the old lathe and other metal objects clearly visible above the blackened rubble.

By the approach of lunchtime, the police sergeant had completed his questioning of fire officers, and Camilla, Roy, Jacob, Fred, Tattoo Trevor plus a few other volunteers. In a sombre voice, he voiced his initial conclusion that this was a deliberate act of arson incorporating the use of an accelerant to create the incident. Meanwhile, it would be some time before restoration work could start while investigations continued.

Camilla, pale and strained, called Roy, Jacob and the others to her side, 'Look everyone, it's been a long night. At least the Hall is ok apart from the drawing room. It'll be out of action until we can go inside and properly assess whatever needs doing. Let's not dwell on that for now, the rest of the building is intact and undamaged, thank God. Please, do come inside and have something to eat and drink.'

They trooped in single file behind Camilla, past the taped-off drawing room. The private lounge at Brompton had changed very little since Camilla moved in. It remained her favourite place on the planet. The same old photographs sat on the sideboard, the speakers on either side of the fireplace were unchanged with, perhaps, a few new additions to the music collection in the yew cabinet where the stereo system stood. The computer desk on the far wall and the bookcase full of trendy magazines were as they always had been. The thick carpet covering the entire floor had survived in immaculate condition despite the occasional wine spillage. The huge television still dominated one of the corners.

A row of grass-stained boots and shoes was lined up on the landing outside the lounge.

Camilla's mobile phone rang out, 'Excuse me everyone, I'll just take this call, it might be the emergency services.'

The men waited in silence.

'Hello, yes Sergeant, how can I help? Yes, I think I already told you, there's quite a number of people who regularly come to the gardens, all volunteers and we employ a couple as well, again as I told you earlier.'

Her eyes were on Jacob as she continued on the phone, 'Yes, of course. I see. Well, Mr and Mrs Elstrop have been with us for several years and are very reliable and... yes, yes. I understand you need to speak to them. Yes, they have keys, but... yes. Well, I understand, of course. Goodbye.'

Camilla cast off her shoes and put her phone away, 'The police want to speak to the Elstrops. I suppose that's perfectly reasonable. I'm afraid Ethel hasn't turned up this morning, and I was relying on her but Roy will rustle up some sandwiches and drinks, he'll be up in a few minutes. Please find a seat.'

Jacob was the first to respond, 'Thank you. I don't think Ethel is very well, Snowy was saying as much to Fred and me.'

'I see. I must say, I was surprised not to see Snowy this morning. He's usually first on the scene for anything out of the ordinary.'

Fred found a seat by the window where he could look out on the walled garden, 'Perhaps, he's looking after his wife.'

Tattoo Trevor was having none of this, 'Bit suspicious if you ask me. You know what Snowy Elstrop is like, always has a gripe against somebody. You wouldn't put it past him, especially if he's had a late one at the Fox and Grape and... well, you know what he's like. He can be a nasty piece of work, can Snowy.'

'Oh, come on now, let's not start speculating. I can't imagine he would…no, it's ridiculous. Let the police do their jobs. It's probably simply another case of wanton vandalism by youngsters and it got out of hand. Who knows?'

Jacob raised an eyebrow, and Camilla looked down at the lush carpet.

'Yes, I know. Sorry. Now I'm speculating.'

Fred turned away from the window, 'I suppose until they start to eliminate people from their enquiries, any one of us will be under suspicion.'

'But who would want to do something like this? I mean, if you were going to take revenge properly, you wouldn't set fire to the shed, you'd damage the Hall…wouldn't you?'

Roy entered the lounge with a wooden trolley, 'What a carry-on, lads, eh? Here, help yourselves.'

'We were just saying. It could be anyone.'

'But who is carrying a grudge? Nobody I can think of, can you?'

Silence filled the room while they contemplated this question and dived into the sandwiches.

Finally, Fred broke the ice, 'Well, I live alone, of course, so I have no alibi. I suppose you're in the same boat, Jacob.'

Tattoo Trevor, his mouth full of ham sandwich, spluttered, 'Well, my wife can vouch for me. We were at home with the family. I slept right through.'

'Look, let's just stop all this. I'm sure the police will catch whoever is responsible. At least I certainly hope they do. Sometimes, these sorts of crimes are difficult to solve. Meanwhile, we must carry on regardless.'

Her phone rang again, 'Hello. Oh, it's you Geoffrey. Yes, thank you. No one injured, we're all accounted for, it's just a question of waiting now. Yes. Yes. Oh yes, I'd almost forgotten about that. Good, yes, well, at east that's something.'

She turned to Jacob, 'That was the Vicar. He said what a good job he managed to collect Miss Bennett's photograph frame otherwise it would have been lost in the fire.'

Jacob smiled and whispered to himself.

'Toconom, toconom.'

CHAPTER TWENTY-ONE

The little framed photograph of the old priest lay under the protection of an old fleece in the well of the front passenger seat of Geoffrey's Volvo. From the car park, he could see Marcia Bennett's pale face at the window as he checked every jacket pocket again. His fingers traced over the wallet in which the picture of the smiling young sailor was safely tucked away. There were no new messages on his mobile phone since he glanced at it, a minute ago.

It rained a little overnight, but the sun was back and the usual people watchers were sitting on their favourite bench. They smiled vacantly as he passed.

Once inside, he pressed the sanitizer dispenser, signed the visitors' book, knocked on Jane Simpson's door and entered her office.

She was speaking into her telephone but, looking up, waved a hand in the air as a signal for him to take a seat, 'Yes, certainly I will…of course…we look forward to seeing you…not at all…any time…bye.'

Geoffrey watched and waited as she scribbled a few notes in a large diary and tapped a few keys on her computer.

The other day, he caught himself imagining Jane and Peter together. They would be awkward with each other at first, that's the way of it when a woman dates a priest. They'd smile a lot and chat about films or favourite music, staying well away from politics and religion. Peter would go heavy with the beer or wine, probably beer, but not too much, just enough to grease the wheels of conversation with a pretty girl. She would be hesitant, at first, but things would warm up as his undoubted charm kicked in.

It wasn't like that when he met Julia; she did all the legwork, making it a lot easier for a shy man with little experience of women. Geoffrey always thought of himself as brave, but not in the manner that others might consider the term.

Peter and Jane would certainly have kissed, passionately Geoffrey imagined, on their first date. Yes, he was convinced of it. What now for them, though?

Jane wrote another item in her diary, then sat back, 'Good to see you, Geoffrey, how are things? Nasty business at Brompton Hall.'

'Hmmm? Oh yes, most unfortunate.'

'Have they charged anyone yet?'

'Not so far as I'm aware. Still making enquiries. That's what they say.'

'Have you come to see Marcia?'

'Yes, how is she doing?'

'Very well. Physically. She's sitting up, and the bruising is fading now, but the fall really shook her up. She's not herself, but that's to be expected. Give it another week and she'll be back to her old self. Come on, I'll take you along to see her.'

'Er no, no. It's ok thanks, I'll go along on my own if you don't mind. I think I need to talk to her on her own, if that's alright with you, Jane.'

Jane turned her attention to the computer screen once more, 'Of course. Let me know if you need anything.'

Earlier today, Geoffrey had gone to the side chapel in St Barnabas's to pray. No one was about, it was very peaceful but, for once, he found it quite difficult. He prayed for the village mostly and, remembering his planned visit to Ramsden House, he'd said a prayer for Marcia Bennett. Yet, it left him unsettled, as though his prayers were simply a checklist of all the up-to-the-minute news and information he could present to the Almighty.

In the corridor, he passed an old gentleman who nodded an unknowing smile in his direction. Geoffrey was embarrassed to admit to himself that it always took a little time to adjust to the smell in this place.

Miss Bennett did not look up when he entered her room, 'Hello my dear, you look well, how are you feeling today?'

Still, she didn't turn to face him, 'I never imagined I would live this long, Vicar. I thought I'd be gone by now. Please sit down, won't you? Thank you for coming to see me, it's good of you to take the time.'

'Nonsense. We're all thinking about you and praying, of course.'

'Tell everybody my condition has stabilised. That's what the doctors told me.'

This was not at all like dear Marcia Bennett. There was a different tone to her voice today, a certain steeliness, 'Would you mind plumping up my pillows? Please. Then we can converse properly.'

'Certainly.'

'They've provided me with a stick, but I can't get the hang of it. I might try again when you've gone. Now then, tell me all about this dreadful business at Brompton Hall. The details, please.'

As Geoffrey recited the events of the previous evening, Miss Bennett sat perfectly erect in her armchair, her eyes on a place far away. When the first question arrived, it took him by surprise.

'Do you think the police know who set fire to the shed?'

'Well, they have charged no one yet.'

'Mmm, that doesn't mean that they don't know the culprit. They require strong evidence to make a case stand up in court.'

'I suppose so.'

One of the carer staff knocked on the door and entered with a tray of tea and biscuits, 'Anything I can get you, Marcia?'

'That's most kind of you, Susan, I think we're fine, what about you Vicar?'

'Please, can we agree on Geoffrey, rather than Vicar?'

Marcia nodded and smiled briefly for the first time since he arrived, 'Yes, of course, and now, what is it you've brought me? As if I didn't know already.'

The blue veins on the back of her hands were prominent in this light, he observed, as she traced the edges of the photo frame with a pale white forefinger. There was no hint of a smile now.

'I think he's done a splendid job, Marcia, don't you?'

Marcia raised an enquiring eyebrow as Geoffrey prattled on, 'Jacob, he's the chap who repaired it. Quite a character, really. Bit of a handyman, seems he can turn his hand to just about anything.'

'Jacob, you say? Ah, the man who is staying in my old cottage. Yes. I am most grateful. Please pass on my thanks, perhaps he will be at St Barnabas's on Sunday? I hope to make it if I can manage this stick by then. They're very good, here, they don't mind taking me.'

They shared a moment of silence to drink some tea.

'No, Marcia, I doubt it somehow, at least I haven't seen him around the church although it's only a couple of weeks, if that, since he turned up in Clamford, so you never know I suppose. Strange thing that, feels as though he's been around for much longer.'

'I miss playing the organ, you know, but with my legs the way they are, it's the pedals do you see?'

She examined the frame, once more, while Geoffrey bit at a digestive, 'When I had my little cottage, I used to look out of the bedroom window. You can see far away up the vale, towards the bridge and the river and way beyond to the hills. Before the storms, I could see who was coming into the village, along the road. The mobile library man used to stop outside every Monday, or was it Tuesday? When they were building the bridge…do you remember that lovely man in charge? Mister Douglas. In the end, I called him Bob. I used to pop up to the building site with snacks. That was fun.'

'I suppose it was.'

'Now, I look out on the car park…not the same, but I'm not one to complain.'

'Marcia.'

'Hmm?'

'There was something else. I'd like to show you.'

Geoffrey delved into his jacket pocket to retrieve his wallet. He placed the photograph of the smiling young sailor in her lap, 'This picture was pressed up against the back of the other one so I thought it best to make you aware. Probably there by mistake…yes?'

Marcia gave in to a deep sigh, 'I'm afraid I didn't sleep at all well in the hospital and I'm weary. Would you mind very much if we called it a day, Geoffrey? I think I might take a nap. It's been lovely to chat, and do please pass on my love to everyone at Clamford. And thank you to Jacob. Most kind.'

'Would you like me to pray with you before I leave?'

'Dear Geoffrey, no need, I think I'm all prayed out.'

CHAPTER TWENTY-TWO

Ted Smailes no longer spent many hours propping up the bar in the Fox and Grape. On the odd lunchtime or early evening when he dropped by, he would be found slumping contentedly in the corner, legs far apart. No, these days, he was more of a listener than a talker. The shed fire was, of course, the only topic in town.

This evening, the bar was busy for such an early hour. The usual suspects, who normally stayed for no longer than half an hour, lingered a little longer at one end next to the dartboard. Ted's sons Phil and Stuart were with Colin and Kenny Sudron, Freddie Bairstow and Peter Stephenson. Judith Balfour, the school headteacher, was sitting in a corner with her junior assistant, Katy, and two white wine spritzers to celebrate a successful end of term concert for the children. The curate clocked Judith's blue beret, which he found curiously alluring. There was a group of bikers at the other end with a few strangers hanging around in the middle. To everyone's surprise, Snowy Elstrop was sitting quietly next to Ted, nursing a pint.

Sandra and Len Hewitt brought out two plates of sandwiches and a bowl of salted peanuts.

'I see Snowy's cutting back a bit, eh? Not surprised, are you? The state he was in! Surprised he's got the nerve to show his face. How Ethel puts up with him is beyond me.'

Len grasped his wife's waist for a cuddle, 'He's a pain in the arse but never knock punters like 'im, they bring in the brass.'

'Well, there's no arguing with that.'

Kenny Sudron had downed three quarters of his pint and was about to quaff the remains and leave when a hand snaked out and took his wrist. His brother, Colin, began his summary of the case for the prosecution.

'I'm telling you, it's dodgy. We had nothing like this lot going on 'till he turns up. I'm not saying he's a wrong'un but, come on guys, Camilla takes him on, just like that, and he's left to his own devices in that shed. Next minute, the thing explodes. He's mucked up, hasn't he? Left something plugged in and it's overheated and triggered a spark or summat and then the paraffin's gone up. Before you know it, the shed's ablaze. Open and shut case if you ask me.'

Peter Stephenson was frowning, his eyes narrow and flitting between Judith Balfour's beret and Len Hewitt's plate of sandwiches, 'Well, for a start, there was nothing to suggest an explosion. So far as I understand, and this is pure speculation, the fire was started by someone deliberately pouring fuel around the shed and setting it alight. Nothing to do with electrics. We shouldn't be pointing fingers is what I'm really saying. Let the police do their job.'

'Fair enough, but I bet I'm not far off the truth.'

It was coming up to six fifteen and the Sudron lads took their leave. Freddie Bairstow remained silent, but the Smailes brothers seemed keen to continue the discussion. Peter noticed that Judith had removed her beret and had ordered another couple of spritzers.

Stuart lowered his voice to a conspiracy whisper, 'You've got to admit, Pete, Col had a fair point, there's a lot of weird stuff gone on since this Jacob bloke arrived. Mind you, our Dad thinks the sun shines out of his arse.'

'Does he really? How very interesting.'

'You taking the piss? Sound like Miss Marple off the telly.'

They fell into a bout of hysterical laughter, which only subsided when the pub door swung open and a police constable walked to the bar, his bright tabard catching the last rays of the low evening sun as he removed his cap and approached Len Hewitt. Sandra smiled, not unkindly, at the young officer and felt a pang of pity for him. Kevin Hindmarsh was no more than a lad with his fresh skin and open face, at once hyper-aware that all eyes had fallen on him.

'Evening Constable, how can I help you?'

Len's gravelly voice seemed to have a slightly reassuring effect on the young man. He rolled his shoulders, resisting the urge, at first, to glance around the bar by keeping his neck and head firm, eyes fixed on Len. Then, slowly, he shifted his stance a little and his peripheral vision picked up Snowy Elstrop's mop of white hair. He turned back to face Len.

'Evening. Sorry to bother you.'

'No problem. Have they caught anyone yet?'

'Still ongoing, but…we're gathering information all the time. I'd like to speak to Mister Elstrop, is he in here this evening?'

Len nodded in the direction of the corner. Ted was enjoying every moment, of course, this was much more like it. Snowy was bolt upright at his side.

'Mister Elstrop?'

'That's me laddie, what's to do?'

'I'd like your assistance, please. I need to ask you a few questions, if that's ok.'

'What about?'

'We don't have to do it here, if you'd like to step outside…or we can go to the police station if you prefer.'

'Can't a man drink in peace these days?'

'Like I said, I'd appreciate your help.'

'Aye, alright. Outside then.'

No one expected this. The evening was over for Snowy and the speculation cranked up a gear.

'What do you make of all that, then?'

Freddie leaned into the question, not knowing what else to say or do. Stuart Smailes shook his head, trying to shake off the fantasy of a drunken Snowy setting light to the shed.

'No way. Not his style. Besides, he might be a raving loony when he's had a few, but Snowy isn't all bad and he isn't a total fool, not daft enough to risk biting the hand that feeds him. The Elstrops do alright out of Brompton Hall, him and Ethel. Doesn't add up.'

'Right on, no motive. And don't forget, he was absolutely paralytic in here before the fire. If you ask me, he was too drunk to stand up, never mind set fire to a shed.'

'Well, why was that young copper fingering him, then?'

'Routine, probably. Only a constable, did you see? Not that sergeant. No detectives. Looks like they don't have a clue.'

Sandra waded in, 'Well, a minute ago, you were all for condemning poor Jacob. I'll say no more...speak of the devil.'

The moment of sudden hush was not lost on Jacob as he surveyed the bar, 'My ears were burning. A beer please, Len.'

'Coming up. Are they still outside?'

'Who do you mean?'

'Snowy and that young constable.'

Jacob played along, content to hold the stage for a while, 'No sign of Snowy, but I saw the police car pull away, maybe he was in it, I didn't see.'

Freddie's jaw dropped a little further, 'Bloody hell! Can they lock him up, just like that, with no proof or anything?'

Sandra came to his rescue, 'No luvvie. They probably just took him home, that's all.'

Jacob gulped down half his beer in one go, 'Sandra's right. Snowy wasn't at Brompton when the police questioned folk, he didn't show. I think Ethel has been under the weather lately. That's all it will be. Just procedure. Him and Ethel have keys for the place. They work most days, so the police will want to talk to them.'

Ted was up out of his seat, 'Jacob's right. Now get your backsides in gear you lads, there are still those beasts to see to, and I want to get that middle stable put right and mucked out properly this time. Fit for a king that should be, fit for a king. Come away.'

'But there's only the old piebald in there, Dad, begging your pardon, Jacob.'

'Fit for a king I said, and fit for a king I meant. Now, crack on.'

Freddie was still a little out of his comfort zone when left in the company of the curate, so he followed the Smailes men out into the evening.

Peter grabbed a handful of peanuts and began to toss them in the air, one at a time, catching them in his open jaws like a pike taking a fly.

Jacob seized his chance, 'So, I meant to ask you. How is that young lady after her fall the other night? I hope she's ok.'

A stray peanut struck Peter's shoulder, 'Oh. You mean Jane. Yes, thank you, fine, fine. No damage done. Thank you for your assistance by the way.'

'No problem.'

Jacob moved over to the corner to finish his drink. Ted's seat was still warm.

Sandra offered Peter a sandwich, 'I bet you have had no tea, am I right? You need to look after yourself, you don't want to end up like some of the regulars with a big beer belly long before your time.'

'You are correct as always, yes, I have not yet eaten and no, I do not wish to acquire a beer belly.'

'How is your lady friend? You know what I mean.'

'Jenny is fine, Sandra. That is to say, so far as I can glean. We haven't seen each other since…'

'Did you call her, like I said?'

'Er, I meant to but, you know how it is, with all that's going on…haven't quite got around to it.'

'Well, why don't you ask her if she'd like to go on a date to that new multiplex at Larchester, there's some good movies on.'

'Yes, I had thought of something along those lines, but then I remembered she said she didn't really enjoy the last time she went to the cinema...too many people on their phones rattling cartons of popcorn. So, that sort of put me off that idea.'

'I wasn't referring to Jane. I think that ship might have sailed, don't you? I meant that lady over there with her friend, from the school, the one with the blue beret. You haven't taken your eyes off her all night.'

Peter looked to the floor, 'I forgot. Nothing gets past you, does it?'

'Very little.'

Nothing seemed to get past Jacob too, sitting alone, the faintest whisper of a word leaving his lips.

CHAPTER TWENTY-THREE

Jacob was not the first to notice that Camilla was not wearing make-up, Tattoo Trevor had already alerted him to the fact. She looked tired and vulnerable in her sweatshirt and jeans, barefooted, her hair tied back in a ponytail.

'Thank you for coming so soon, Detective Constable Hindmarsh, I appreciate it. This is all very difficult, and it probably seems melodramatic to you but I want it this way. You've met the people here I think, you interviewed each of them. Their presence isn't an accident. I want this whole business out of the way so that we can move on properly. So, please, you said on the phone that you had some important information…'

Roy stood at her side, serious and pale, arms folded across his chest, jaw set rigid and tense. Fred was sitting nervously by the window, his hands tugging occasionally at his trousers, looking at Jacob for some sort of reassurance.

'Thank you, Miss Wilberforce. I'll keep this brief. Following our enquiries into the fire, we arrested and charged someone with criminal damage and arson, intending to cause damage. That person is an employee here by the name of Ethel Elstrop.'

'Whoa!...you mean her husband, surely?'

'No Miss. She has made a full confession.'

'But how did she do it? In the middle of the night? And, more importantly…why?'

'I cannot answer that question at the moment.'

'Then, how can you be so sure that it was Ethel? She's been ill, she could be covering for someone.'

'She's not covering for her husband, if that's what you're implying Mister Sudron. I interviewed the Elstrops at their home. Her husband wanted to take the blame, at first, but she was having none of it. She owned up straight away. Her account of the incident, and her injuries, all added up.'

'Her injuries?'

'She was in some discomfort and very distressed, there were burns to her hands and wrists. We are getting her admitted to hospital.'

'Bloody Hell! This gets crazier by the minute.'

Kevin Hindmarsh's shoulders seemed to relax a little, 'As you know, we are taking these sorts of crime very seriously indeed. Someone could have been badly injured, or worse. Have you any idea why she might have done this, Miss? Any of you? Was there trouble brewing? An argument, a dispute that got out of hand?'

'What are you saying? Ethel hasn't told you why she did it?'

'Not a peep.'

Fred rose from his seat by the window, 'This is dreadful. Can I make a suggestion? Perhaps it's possible that the poor woman had some sort of breakdown. Her husband, Snowy, did say something about her not being herself lately.'

'Thank you. We have asked for medical reports but, in the meantime, if there's anything that occurs to any of you…any reason she might have acted this way, get in touch. We are still talking to her husband, but we're getting nothing from him. We have a crime, we have the perpetrator and a full confession, but we don't have a motive.'

'Right. I see.'

Detective Constable Kevin Hindmarsh remembered his training and waited for his words to hang a little longer in the warmth of the lounge, 'Well, I need to get back to the station. Thank you for your assistance. Miss Wilberforce, can I have a word in private before I go, thanks.'

Camilla saw Hindmarsh out of the lounge and silence descended on the men.

Fred fiddled with the turn-up of one of his trouser legs and inhaled long and deep through his nose. A word was trying to escape his moving lips, but Jacob's watchful eyes prevented it. The look said don't.

Roy stood, arms folded again, by the window, like a sentry.

Tattoo Trevor's eyes were everywhere. He liked this room, very much. The combination of warm colours, exotic artifacts and expensive furniture cast a seductive spell that he couldn't resist. Many times, when toiling in the gardens or even at the allotments, he had found himself alone, speculating on the interior of Brompton. The reality surpassed his limited imagination. Yet, this was not a forbidding, scary place in the least. Sure, it was the sort of room where you take your shoes off before coming in, without having to be asked, but it was also inviting and comfortable. Everything in here, from the photographs to the ornaments and the yew furniture, was spotless and immaculate. Ethel must do an excellent job.

Trevor stretched in the armchair before deciding to stand to his full height, he wanted to explore. The carpet was soft and yielded to his heavy tread as he moved towards the two large vases at the window. Then, mid journey, something attracted him to the bookcase. A couple of hypnotic abstract paintings drew him even closer. Several piles of glossy magazines adorned the very top shelf and, under one of them, the frayed edge of something vaguely familiar was protruding. His eyes remained fixed on it while he feigned interest in a racing magazine by flicking through a few pages. Then, he let his finger roam where it would, ever so gently, until it found the frayed material.

'You dropped something on the carpet.'

Fred's soft voice brought a little glow of cheer to the others.

'Have I? Where?'

Roy unfolded his arms and pointed to a piece of folded paper, lying in the centre of the carpet.

'Oh yeah. Thanks,'

Trevor stooped low to retrieve it. He didn't bother to look at it but shoved it hard into the back pocket of his jeans, then returned to his chair, just as Camilla re-entered. Her cheeks seemed to have recovered some of their former colour.

'Ok. Well, that was all a bit of a shock, wasn't it? Look guys, I can't thank you enough for your support and help, but I've got a lot of business to deal with, as you can imagine. I'm told we can now get on with hiring a skip for the rubbish, so Roy will crack on with that. I don't think there's any more we can achieve in here. Roy, will you please see that the guys all have a drink before they go, there's plenty in the downstairs kitchen? Thanks. And thanks again to all of you. At least, we can now start to put all this behind us. Pick up the pieces as it were…'

She appeared on the verge of tears, 'Oh, and please. I'm sure I don't really have to remind you but, you know, news travels fast and soon enough everyone in the Vale will know what's happened. Can I just ask that we all…you know…if we're asked about it all, as we will be…that we are careful and a little…'

Fred was quick to help her out.

'Circumspect.'

'Circumspect. Absolutely.'

The men filed out, one by one, collecting their boots and shoes on the way. Trevor was last in the line, and at the door, turned to face Camilla.

'Camilla, can I? No doesn't matter, I can see you're upset.'

'No, no. Go on. You were going to say something.'

'Well, I was wondering. Do you remember that day at the allotments when you came over, after little Barney passed away, God rest his soul? You remember we were looking through all his stuff in that quaint shed of his? Like an Aladdin's cave.'

'Of course I remember. That little chap was a great comfort to me at just the right moment after Aunt Harriett died.'

'Well, the thing is. I notice, like, you have one of them there files up there on the shelf.'

'Yes, I keep it as a fond memory of a kind man.'

'Well, the thing is. Will it be alright if, whenever, I could look at it. Just out of interest…to remember, like?'

'Well yes, of course, that'll be fine, but not now. I have so much to do. But remind me…yes?'

'Thanks. Appreciate that.'

Trevor nodded his goodbye, picked up his boots at the door and carried them downstairs to the fresh air of the gardens. He felt about in his back pocket and removed the piece of folded paper on which was written the word TOCONOM.

CHAPTER TWENTY-FOUR

Geoffrey felt another rush of panic and swallowed hard, 'This will need handling with great sensitivity. It will send shockwaves through the village, believe me.'

'Geoff, I do believe you but, all I'm saying is this...do you not think there's a great danger that people will get things out of all proportion? Talking to the guys in the Fox and Grape, you'd think it was the crime of the century. I mean to say, look, it's a nasty business that shouldn't have happened and the police have to do their job and be seen to be doing it, I get all of that but...it's only a burned-out old shed. No one was seriously hurt. Least said, soonest mended and all that.'

Geoffrey glared at his curate, shook his head, and slammed his diary shut. He would do the right thing, he would listen to other voices, of course he would, because that was his job, but he would not indulge the sort of childish, sentimental tosh that masquerades too often as compassion and a misguided distortion of the truth.

'Have you learned nothing? Only a burnt-out old shed, eh? Peter, there have been Elstrops in these parts since Adam was a lad. They are part of the fabric of this little community, always there, noisy but harmless, imperfect but tolerable, like the changing seasons. Now, they have been found to be something else, something else altogether.'

'What, exactly?'

'Not to be trusted, sinister and dangerous.'

'This is Snowy and Ethel we're talking about.'

Geoffrey's palm slammed on the desk, 'If you want to keep your job, you will do well never to patronise me again, ever!'

Peter felt the surge of blood pumping through his skull to his ears. His head weighed a ton and flopped forward, 'Wow! I think it's best if I leave you alone.'

Geoffrey's arm shot out to grasp the curate's wrist tight, 'Stay!'

Silence hung like a heavy shroud over the two priests.

'You didn't deserve that. Forgive me. We must stay together on this. But you must try to understand the nature of the business we are dealing with.'

'Yes. So, what do you think we should do, exactly?'

'First, we must pray. And we must listen and we must think. Something is afoot in this village, and I don't understand its nature, but I can feel it. Most of all, we must stick together. Let's go first to the Church, then I think we'll pay a call at Ramsden House to see Marcia, the drive over there will give us a bit of breathing space to consider everything.'

'Oh…right.'

'Problem?'

'No, not at all.'

'Right then.'

Geoffrey always made it clear to the Parochial Church Council that Saint Barnabas's must remain open through the day, so that the building was always seen as a welcoming place for the locals to visit. In the event, few people in Clamford were given to private prayer, and the building was often unoccupied for many hours at a time. Doubtless, in view of recent events, there would be renewed calls for a policy review. Today, there were only a couple of strangers at prayer in the front row pews, they spent a few minutes for reflection, signed the visitors' book next to the font, and departed. Geoffrey and Peter nodded as the visitors left the building before heading to the side chapel.

An hour and a half later, they arrived at Ramsden Care Home, there is no sign of Marcia Bennett at her bedroom window.

'Who have you come to see?'

'Marcia Bennett.'

'Right. Well, they're all in the dining room having their lunch.'

The young woman held her smile and stared at Peter for a few seconds too long, 'If you're waiting for Jane, she isn't here, there's a meeting at Head Office.'

'Thank you, we'll wait in Miss Bennett's room while she's having her lunch, if you'd be kind enough to inform her. Please. No need to rush, let her enjoy her lunch. Thanks.'

'Sure. No problem.'

The girl's voice was cheerful and direct with a hint of Irish mischief or maybe Scottish, Geoffrey was undecided. What was certain was that her blunt message was music to Peter's ears. By the time they reached Marcia's room, Geoffrey's curiosity defeated him.

'Do I detect a little turbulence on the romantic front?'

'Don't catch your drift.'

'I thought you and Jane were an item. Julia mentioned something about a pasta meal?'

'Can we change the subject, please?'

Unable to coax even the trace of a smile from Peter, Geoffrey allowed himself a few moments to take some pleasure in his curate's obvious discomfort, 'To what exactly?'

'Pardon?'

'What do you want to talk about?'

Peter sat down on the end of Marcia's bed, hands on knees, 'How is Hilda getting on at the school?'

The moment of pleasure fled from Geoffrey as quickly as it had arrived, 'Low blow...even for you.'

'No, I'm not being mean. I think she's a great kid, I'm just interested, that's all. Do you have much contact with the Head, what's she like?'

'Judith Balfour? Very good, I believe. Only met her a couple of times. Seems very pleasant, quite engaging. Sense of humour.

Julia thinks highly of her if that's anything to go by. Why do you ask?'

'No particular reason. Seen her out and about, on the odd occasion.'

'Aha…now I see…'

There was sudden activity in the corridor which put an end to the conversation, then a loud tap on the door made Geoffrey jump to attention. When he opened it, Marcia was just about to give it another thwack with her walking stick.

'I can't quite manage to work the door handle and hold on to my stick and keep my balance all at the same time. Hello Vicar, Geoffrey, how lovely to see you, and you too, Peter. I am honoured, both of you are together. Am I about to die or something? What have you heard?'

Geoffrey stood awkwardly and guided her through the threshold, but Peter appreciated the joke with a good belly laugh. He leapt from the bed to help Marcia to her chair by the window, 'You look terrific, actually. Much brighter, I must say, doesn't she, Geoff?'

'Much brighter, yes.'

'Thank you, I'm feeling much stronger. And how are you two, today? What news do you bring? Have they caught them, the people who caused the fire?'

'Oh, I expect you'll hear it all soon enough. That's partly why we've both come along. I'm afraid the news will come as a shock, we're all shocked. The police arrested and charged Ethel Elstrop; it seems she deliberately started it.'

'She made a full confession.'

They waited for the obvious question, but it didn't come, neither did any signs of shock or repugnance.

Peter couldn't put his finger on why her expression unnerved him. Why was there no attitude of surprise? She didn't know the Elstrops that well; it was true, but all the same…it was almost as if she was expecting this. Or was it just an old age thing? Would the old girl suddenly burst into tears at any moment?

'They have no idea why she did it. She won't say.'

Marcia turned to Geoffrey, 'She acted alone?'

'So it seems.'

'I see.'

'Can we get you a cup of tea, Marcia?'

'No thank you, I'm quite full. It was quite a substantial lunch, not at all unpleasant. But, if *you* want one, I'm sure they'll be happy to bring you one. What about you, Peter? A cup of tea?'

'No, no, we're fine, thanks.'

'Well, I expect the entire village will have heard the news by now. Thank you for coming to inform me. These things can be very disconcerting, can't they? Destabilising. In a small community like Clamford.'

'Quite.'

Marcia noticed Geoffrey's eyes as they took in the photograph frame, which had been returned to its customary place on the small table beside the bed, 'Thank you again for getting my picture repaired. And for the other little photograph. I know you are both interested in knowing who these two characters are, aren't you? Well, it's none of your business…'

She started to giggle. Marcia Bennett was not one to giggle, ever. Lovely woman, though she most certainly was, Geoffrey had long acknowledged that she was not a person who easily succumbed to levity.

'But I'm going to tell you, anyway. You see, sitting here in this room, day after day, looking out of the window, thinking of times past…well, God has given me a wonderful opportunity to reflect and to…reconsider.'

'Have you been very miserable here, my dear?'

'At first. Certainly. But, not anymore. Not today. Listen up, both of you. I'm going to tell you a story. I used to love telling stories to the children at the village school and I think I was rather good at it. I should have kept at it, but I didn't. I was born in Larchester, just after the start of the war. My father was in charge of the bank, mother came from good stock and didn't work, we were well-off; I was an only child. A very respected family. You could say, I was sheltered and spoiled, but mother said I always had a good heart and a kind spirit. I don't know about that.'

'I'm sure she was correct.'

'When I was sixteen, that would be in nineteen fifty-seven, I was invited to a local dance by the daughter of someone known to father. My parents relented, and I was allowed to go. It was *very* exciting. I had never seen or heard the like of it. It was fun. Intoxicating. I met a man, older than I was but young in appearance and spirit, good looking, funny. He was called Arthur. I fell in love, and in weeks, I was pregnant. Everything stopped from that moment. My young man disappeared, of course. Mother hid herself away while father got to work.'

Geoffrey had heard confessions many times, some were far more lurid than Marcia's but this was the first to make him sweat, 'That must have been a very hard time.'

'Oh, it was. I was sent away to the Midlands to have my child, on my own. A private place, I expect it cost a fortune. It was a boy. My parents, both of them, arranged for the child to be sent to a children's home for future adoption. I had no say in the matter. My father took care of everything, money wise, and I was very, very frightened. My mother softened a little, and it was suggested that I should move away to study. Eventually, I chose to go into teaching. I have never regretted entering education, it has been my salvation.'

'You were so young. Did no one else help you?'

Marcia pointed to the picture of the old priest.

'He did. The Reverend Henry Cattermole. He was kind and gentle. Helped to pacify my father. It was he who helped to take care of arrangements for my child. I recall that I had to sign a document to say that I would not attempt to have any further contact with the child. Henry took me under his wing and brought me to the church, he was very kind when I needed kindness. People could be very judgemental in those days. Having a baby out of wedlock was a thing that didn't happen to decent girls. I kept this photograph of him hidden away for a long time, but then, living on my own, what did it matter? It's been with me for years. Henry Cattermole. I take comfort in that picture.'

'What happened to the child's father…Arthur?'

'Huh! I never saw him again. But, one day, it would be in the early seventies I suppose, I received a plain envelope through my door. Inside was a photograph of a young sailor; a happy young man with an open smile. I knew in an instant that it was a photograph of my child, grown up. Call it a mother's instinct. His eyes were like his father's, twinkling and full of life. I never found out who delivered that envelope, maybe Henry Cattermole delivered it, I don't know, and I didn't get the opportunity to find out if it was indeed Henry. I discovered in Parish notices that he died rather suddenly soon after. I decided to keep the little photo hidden, behind the picture of my priest. It felt right to keep them together. And there it stayed.'

'Until your accident, in here.'

Marcia nodded quietly.

'Did you ever…?'

'Try to find him? No. He looked so happy. Why would I go charging back into his life? In any case, you must remember, this was in the days before the internet, there was no contact list. I did hope, once or twice, that curiosity might make him wish to search for the woman who brought him into this world. Like one sees on that television programme about long- lost families. But no.'

Peter looked down at his feet, 'That's quite a story. I feel very humbled that you've told us all of this.'

'And now you are asking yourself a few questions, aren't you? Well, let me head them off. The answer to the first is no, I have told my tale to no one else. The answer to the second is: I told you this today because I believe it's very important to remind oneself that one must never judge simply by appearances. The woman you knew me as yesterday is not the person you see before you, here today. Yet here I am, still Miss Marcia Bennett, spinster of this parish, beloved retired teacher and church organist who never strays from the right path. Nothing has changed, yet it has. One never truly knows what's going on in people's lives. Who knows what made Ethel Elstrop start that fire? So there you are, that should satisfy your curiosity. You both look concerned for me, but don't be. Please. I don't deserve it and I don't need it. An enormous burden of guilt and secrecy has been lifted. I'm free of it after all these years of hidden shame and regret. I'm free because someone set fire to a shed. What do they say? It's an ill wind that blows no one any good.'

'What wise words. Thank you, Marcia.'

'Now, I'm a little tired after my lunch. It's been lovely to see you both, please give my love to everyone and I hope to see them very soon. Take care.'

CHAPTER TWENTY-FIVE

The skip was ugly and enormous, its deep yellow paintwork incongruous in the quiet garden where Jacob and Tattoo Trevor were both stripped to the waist in the warm morning sun, heavy duty gloves covering their hands.

'You start over there, Trev. I'll shift this lot, as best I can. Between us, we can make a decent start I reckon. Fred, don't you go lifting anything heavy, mind. There's plenty of other jobs need doin'.'

The big yellow beast seemed to give out a mighty echo of protest with each load of heavy, charred timber that was slung away into its deep, empty bowels.

Fred took himself off to the shade of the sycamore for a chat to one or two of the volunteers and a group of nosey parkers who had come to see the damage for themselves, while Trevor and Jacob worked through the first half hour without a break. Jacob couldn't remember a time when he needed a clock, he'd worked in the open air for so many years, season after season, he could almost tell the time by the movement of the birds in the trees. Today, the birds were keeping their distance.

'You ready for a break, Jacob? I brought some tea in my flask.'

'Right, thanks.'

They peered over the rim of the yellow skip; the bottom was barely covered with the rubbish they'd managed to remove, so far. Trevor rubbed a heavy glove across his chest, his growing respect for the older man reaching new heights, 'Shit, this is going to take longer than I thought. How are you doing?'

'Don't be worrying about me, lad. I'm just fine. We'll get through it, you'll see.'

The faint stench of smoke damaged timber, burned out roof felt and old ashes still lingered around the skip, so they settled for a spot in the shade of the main wall where they could see the entire spread of the larger garden and smell the pine needles; it was not long before Fred joined them.

'One of my kids made this tea, it tastes alright after the first mouthful.'

'My Evelyn made a good cup of tea.'

Jacob chuckled to himself, 'Well, we got the sun, the sky, the air…who cares if the tea's not perfect?'

Fred doffed his cap at Jacob, 'Very true.'

Fred wished he could do what Jacob just did; he could come up with the right thing to say at just the right time to make everything feel a little better. People rarely take kindly to folk who tell the truth, plain and simple. They scoff away at them, speak ill behind their back, but not with Jacob. Everyone seemed to like him and believe him, somehow.

Jacob flicked away a fly, 'How many Tattoos have you got, Trev?'

'Lost count, to be honest. Not that many. You do daft things when you're young.'

'Best time to do them.'

'Yeah, you're right there. No good havin' regrets, mind you. Best thing that happened to me was marrying my lass. She sorted me out. Never looked back. Lovely bairns as well, I'm a lucky bugger.'

'Evelyn and me, we couldn't have children but we were happy as larks. It's good to look back and be able to smile.'

Jacob made a move to stand up, suddenly and unexpectedly, as if he'd discovered he'd lost something from his pockets. His eyes scanned the expanse of garden, from the sycamore to the far walls and gravel paths, 'Have you two noticed 'owt different?'

'Eh? What do you mean?'

'Have a good look around.'

Fred and Trevor got to their feet in silence.

'Well?'

'Nothing unusual.'

'Nope.'

'Where's Arthur?'

'Arthur?'

'The scarecrow. He's gone. Just disappeared. I never noticed 'till just now.'

'Yeah, you're right. Last week, he was right there in the middle of the fruit bushes.'

'That's right, but…'

'Why would a scarecrow disappear?'

'It was nowhere near the shed.'

'Well, it wouldn't move on its own.'

'What do you reckon?'

'I reckon Ethel must have grabbed it out of the ground and chucked it into the fire.'

'Why the hell would she do summat like that?'

'Who knows? Crazy moment of madness?'

'Daft I call it. I remember that old scarecrow down at the allotments when old Barney…bloody hell, I just thought of summat.'

'What?'

Trevor looked concerned, worried even; it was a look that didn't sit well on his usual face and it unsettled the other two men.

'The scarecrow. That old picture you found when you fixed up the frame. I'm not sure about it, but...I'll have to have a word with Camilla.'

'Camilla? What's it got to do with her?'

'I need to be sure.'

'What about?'

'Nowt really...except. Never mind me, I'll tell you later. Probably me getting things mixed up. Forget it. Let's crack on getting this lot shifted!'

As the day meandered into late afternoon, Trevor wished he had not brought up the subject of the little framed photograph, it only increased this weird sense of foreboding. Tomorrow, he would get back to his allotment and he'd put more shifts in for the delivery company. He'd spent enough time in this garden lately. In truth, he'd be glad to see the back of the damned skip.

'You're quiet Trevor, what's up my friend?'

'Oh! Don't fret about me, man. Summat on my mind, that's all. I'm gonna knock off now for the day. Glad we got it all shifted.'

Jacob slapped him on the back at the place where a small anchor marked Trevor's shoulder blade, 'I won't be far behind you. Where's Fred?'

'Over by the fruit trees. There's only us three left, the others have long gone.'

Trevor slung his backpack over his shoulder and collected his bike on the way to the gravel path. As soon as he was out of sight of the others, he paused. There was no sign of the Land Rover by the house. Why wouldn't this stupid sense of unease loosen its grip? It was annoying; he had to shake it off, or he'd end up taking it home to the kids and he was not having that. He propped the bike against the side wall of the house and knocked on the big front door. It took less than a minute for it to open.

'Oh, it's you, Trevor. I wasn't expecting anyone, what can I do for you? How has it gone today with the skip?'

'Sorry to bother you, Camilla, can I come in? Won't take long, promise.'

'Of course you can. Come on up.'

The private lounge was bathed in the low light of early evening.

'I won't sit down, thanks, I'm covered in dust and stuff. I just wanted to ask you summat, like.'

'Ok, I'm listening. Is it about that old file I keep in here? You asked if you could have a look at it.'

'Yeah. Well, sort of. You remember that old photograph frame that Jacob fixed up for Miss Bennett? And the little picture of the sailor. Remember?'

'What of it?'

'Did it remind you of anyone?'

Camilla recharged her glass of red wine, 'Join me?'

'No thanks, I have to get off home.'

She quaffed the wine in a single go and reached up to the top shelf of the bookcase to retrieve the old file with the frayed edges, 'I think I'm one jump ahead of you, Trevor.'

'What do you mean?'

'It is Barney, isn't it? The sailor in the picture. Either that or it's his twin brother. A younger version than you and I knew him, but otherwise, identical. The eyes, everything. Him.'

'So, it's not just me, then?'

Camilla began to leaf through the pages of the old file, 'He was an amazing little man. I'll never forget him. That day, when you and I went to his little cabin thing by the allotments, I often think about that.'

'Yeah, so do I.'

'So sad when he just passed away like that. I learned so much from him. So much. When I first wandered down there, past that woman with the dungarees and the yellow hat, remember her?'

'She's still around, with the same hat.'

'And you were there of course, and you pointed me toward this weird little man. A common man, simple you might say, but simple in a good way. Not stupid. Wise. There was nothing threatening about him. Nothing. He gave me tea, and it tasted wonderful. And Arthur was his scarecrow.'

Trevor bowed his head at the memories as she continued, 'Barney told me about clouds and the weather. I thought I knew it all back then. I had an opinion on everything. The more I learned in the city, or thought I'd learned, the more arrogant I became, and the more angry, and self-righteous. My aunt Harriet was the only one who really understood me. Until I listened to Barney. Good old Barney. He couldn't talk about anything intellectual or philosophical with me, not really. At first, I just dismissed him as some sort of country bumpkin. But he was strangely mesmerising, down to earth, in a common-sense way. He didn't browbeat me, but he spoke with such a simple love of life. He spoke with conviction and assurance, the sort that I thought I had, but discovered I did not. It wasn't just his voice or even his words, there was something magical going on. Our relationship, such as it was, too brief, was very unlikely, but I hung on every word he spoke. I used to complicate everything, but he taught me differently. I wanted all the answers. He taught me to accept and see things simply, as they are.'

'Arthur, the scarecrow is gone. In the fire.'

'What? How?'

'Dunno, but Jacob reckons Ethel must have chucked him on the fire when she set the shed alight.'

'But why?'

Trevor shrugged and trod as lightly as he could manage over the thick carpet to where Camilla was examining the old file.

'Switch on that light, will you, by the desk, it's getting a little darker in here.'

Camilla placed the file on the smart yew desk and skimmed through some more of the old pages. To one side, stood a highly polished double-sided reading mirror with a flexible handle which Harriet used during her later years.

'Hold on. There…stop.'

Trevor placed a large hand on the page in question.

'There…look.'

Camilla looked a little closer.

'Orchids. They must have been his favourite plant. The drawings are exquisite, must have taken ages to produce this lot. Every detail. Beautiful.'

'Hold the mirror closer, like that, where it'll catch the light again. Now…see it? See the title across the top?'

'THE MONOCOT FAMILY. That is the proper name given to orchids. I remember when we looked at this page together, the day Barney died.'

'In the mirror there, you can catch the reflection off the light. See it now? Backwards, it reads… TOCONOM. See? TOCONOM.'

'And your point is…?'

Trevor was about to reply when a loud crack rang out from somewhere close.

'Hear that?'

'Car back firing, probably. Noise travels.'

Another crack. This time they leaped away, and Trevor pressed a hand against the window frame. A figure flitted across the periphery of their vision, in the walled garden.

'I think that was Fred I just saw. No, I'm sure of it. Just caught a glimpse. Summat's up. Better go down there.'

'I'll follow you.'

The light was fading quite fast now, the shadow from the house had already spread over much of the lawns as they dashed round the corner, along the gravel path to the walled garden. They turned, at speed, towards the sound of urgent cries.

Trevor spotted Fred first, crouching down close to the big yellow skip, and sprinted towards him. Camilla put her hands to her face in shock. The warm sun, dipping down under the trees, was surely playing terrible tricks on them. There was something over there: a body, another body.

The twisted body of a man was sprawled against the side of the skip where a huge dark stain had formed, dripping, dark against the hideous yellow metal. A shapeless mass of shattered bone, tissue and human pulp had replaced the space occupied by the man's head, just seconds ago. In its lifeless hands, the body was holding a shotgun; it pointed to the reddening sky.

Fred was moaning now as he knelt over the second body, cradling it in his arms and rocking it gently backwards and forwards.

Trevor called out, 'Camilla! Don't come near! Go back to the house, call an ambulance. Fetch Roy. I'll stay here with Fred and Jacob. Go quickly!'

'Jacob?'

'He's been shot in the chest. Run!'

PART TWO

THE DEPARTURE

CHAPTER TWENTY-SIX

From the passenger seat of his unmarked car, Phil Butterfield tried to work out how many years had passed since he was last in Clamford; must be two years and a bit, just after the statue hoo-ha, but the old place never changed much. He flicked away a few crumbs from his sports jacket, wiped a tissue across his moustache and closed the lid on his Tupperware box.

'Did I tell you, Kevin? Kath's got me on a diet, tuna and cucumber today. She says she wants me fit for next year when we go on a cruise. Got it all worked out, she has.'

'Won't be the same without you, Sir.'

'You can count on that. Still, all good things come to an end, Constable.'

Phil Butterfield had been around the block more times than anyone could count. He knew his patch; he loved this part of the world, the people, their towns and villages, their land. Now in the twilight of his career, his keen eye and his old-style instincts were as sharp and perceptive as they ever were.

Another frown creased his brow. This sort of madness did not happen in Clamford. In the twenty-four hours since the major incident at Brompton Hall, the village had been stunned into a state of cold shock and sad desperation. He'd seen this sort of stuff many times in this part of the north but never imagined it could happen here. Now, he'd been landed with the investigation; not that you could really call it an investigation. It wasn't the usual 'who dunnit?' was it?   More like a 'why do it?' He knew why they'd given him the case: open and shut, just a few loose ends to tie up. Something to keep the old boy busy before he finally retired.

All the same, this case had got him interested. Why would a well-known local, part of the very fabric of the place, suddenly want to shoot another man at close range and then turn his weapon on himself and blow his brains out? Where's the motive? What sort of passion and desperation got into a man's head to make him want to do that? In Clamford of all places. What a turnaround in just a few days, from being a place where folk came for some peace and amusement, "to have a butchers at the naked lady statue", this village had been transformed overnight. His team of cops were knocking on doors, trained councillors had been despatched to the school and the vicar, Geoffrey Roper, had arranged for a church pastoral team to support distressed residents. Perhaps the vicar would come up with some answers, if he really knew his flock.

'I'll talk to the Reverend Roper later on. Any news on this Jacob fella?'

Detective Superintendent Butterfield already knew the answer to this question, but it paid to keep young coppers like Constable Kevin Hindmarsh on their toes, to make sure no time was lost in getting to the bottom of this madness.

'No boss. Still unconscious, but the doctors at Larchester Hospital reckon he's stable. The next few hours are critical. As soon as he wakes up…'

'IF he wakes up.'

'If he wakes up, they'll let us know. We've covered most of the locals, but we're not getting very much from them. Everyone's in shock and nobody can shed much light on why it's happened.'

'Aye lad. Just go over it one more time. Tell me again. What's in the statement from the old chap, Fred. He's the key witness.'

Phil Butterfield remembered every word of the statement, but these old methods had never let him down and he trusted them now, they would prove their worth. If heard the words spoken aloud, they might trigger an idea that was worth a follow up.

'I haven't got the statement with me, Boss, but...'

'Just say out loud what you can remember.'

'Well, he was under the sycamore in the walled garden at Brompton Hall, getting ready to pack in for the evening. He had half an eye on Jacob, who looked pretty tired. It had been a long day, they were all looking forward to seeing the back of that skip, so they could put the fire incident behind them. Trevor Matthews had gone home, as far as Fred knew. That's the tall guy with the tattoos.'

'I know who Trevor Matthews is, go on.'

'Next thing he knew, there's Snowy Elstrop, shouting and bawling. Fred reckons Snowy must have come up the back way by the narrow path along the river bank because he certainly didn't see him come round by the house. Mister Elstrop was shouting at Jacob and waving something in his hand. Then he saw it was a rifle. Jacob was talking low-like to him, trying to calm him down. Fred said that he couldn't really make out what

Snowy was shouting, but he sounded furious. Then the shots went off and Jacob fell forward.'

'Right. What did Fred do?'

'He said he couldn't help himself, he started to run as fast as his legs would carry him towards Snowy, Mister Elstrop. He said he probably shouted something, but he can't remember. All he could see was Snowy looking back at him with the rifle in his arms. After that, it was so quick, he just shoved the thing under his chin and pulled the trigger, just like that.'

'That must have terrified Fred.'

'Yes Sir. He said it was the most terrible thing he'd ever seen. He said he just started crying and ran to Jacob and held him. Jacob's eyes flickered a bit but then closed and that's when the other two witnesses arrived.'

'Trevor Matthews and Camilla Wilberforce.'

'Yes, Sir. That's the gist of it.'

'Have you interviewed Ethel Elstrop again, like I said?'

'Yes, Sir, but she's not saying anything new.'

'Keep at her, she must know a lot more than she's letting on. I want to speak to this Trevor guy again. After Fred, he was next on the scene after the shots were fired. He might have forgotten something. Now, sit there and tell me what you see, Constable.'

'You mean right now?'

'Right now.'

'Everything I see?

'Aye.'

'Well, I see the river over there and the bridge. In the distance, I can see the start of the cottages and the church steeple but I can't see any tracks and there doesn't seem to be anyone around at the minute, it's quiet. And I can see the statue of the naked lady over there.'

'Good, anything else?'

'Not sure there is much else, Sir.'

'Look up.'

Kevin Hindmarsh leaned forward in the driver's seat and screwed up his eyes to shield from the bright morning sunshine as he craned his neck towards the sky.

'Hardly a cloud, just blue sky.'

'Exactly. A beautiful day in Clamford, but no one's about. Ever since that day when they put up that statue of Harriet Wilberforce, you'll find visitors coming here from all over. Especially on days like this. They stop to admire the lady in the buff, cross over the road bridge, maybe stop at the Fox and Grape, have a look around the village and move on. That statue's been the making of this place. Now, it's quiet. You see, something like this shooting isn't just another violent crime, it's got a life of its own. It has roots that go down deep and they find their way into people's lives. Ordinary people. It destabilises them. We have to find where those roots are and dig them out, bring them out into the open.'

'Yes, Sir.'

'So…start digging. You talk to Ethel Elstrop again and I'll speak to Trevor Matthews.'

CHAPTER TWENTY-SEVEN

Tattoo Trevor shook his head, his eyes trying to take in his surroundings, but, so far as he could see, there were only bare walls, a couple of hard chairs, and a desk.

'Thanks for coming in, has anyone offered you a cuppa yet?'

'I'm fine, thanks. Will this take long? I know nowt more than I already put in my statement. I need to get back to work.'

'We won't keep you any longer than necessary and let me say straight away that you are not in any kind of trouble. The opposite. We are very grateful for your assistance. So, thanks for your statement, Mister Matthews, may I call you Trevor? Thanks Trevor. You've been extremely helpful, this must have been a terrible experience for you.'

'I still can't take it all in. I get home, talk to the wife, the kids, the dog, and then my mind goes back to it. Sometimes, I shake, you know?'

'I understand. Are you getting any help? Maybe see your doctor, get some counselling, that often helps.'

'Nah. But thanks. I might think about it.'

'You do that. Look, Trevor, I don't want to make this any harder for you but it's important we try to establish all the facts, we need to understand why this happened, so that the whole sorry business can be put to bed and everyone can move on.'

'Is that what they mean when they say closure?'

'Exactly. So, let's just have a chat, you and me, see if there's anything more that might help us with that. Something you might have forgotten, some tiny detail, anything. Ok?'

'Aye. Fine.'

'So how well did you know the Elstrops?'

'Everyone knows Snowy and Ethel. They're proper characters and you have to take them as you find them, know what I mean? Can't believe he's gone. Snowy was always in your face about something or other, he could start an argument in an empty room but once you got used to his ways, then he wasn't really so bad. I'll say this about the pair of them: they were good workers. Ethel worked mainly in the big house and Snowy helped her out, but often you'd find him in the gardens. He liked folk to know that him and Ethel were well thought of by Harriet Wilberforce, God rest her soul. He thought she was wonderful and, to be fair, she must have known how to handle them both. Ethel stuck up for Snowy and vice versa, they looked after each other. He was a man's man, always in the pub, usually drunk by the end of the night and that's when you had to be careful, like. He enjoyed winding people up when he'd had a drink. Roy Sudron once lost his cool and gave him a right belting, but it soon blew over. That was Snowy; he could be an aggravating little bugger, but he meant no harm, not really. Ethel just went along with him, that's how they were.'

'And when this Jacob arrived on the scene, how did Snowy take to him?'

'What do you mean?'

'Well, did they have arguments? Did they get on? Can you think of anything that might have led to him wanting to shoot him?'

'I can't…honest. I can't figure any of it out. I mean, we all knew Snowy had been quiet lately, not himself like, but we put that down to Ethel being unwell. Like I said to you, they were a strong couple. He took time off to look after her.'

'So, are you telling me that Snowy Elstrop and this Jacob got on well?'

Trevor ran his forefinger along his nose and thought long and hard about his response while Butterfield leaned back in his chair, waiting, thumbs tucked into the pockets of his green cardigan.

'Well, I wouldn't go that far but, now I come to think on it, he took to Jacob as well as he took to anyone else. This is a close-knit community, Mister Butterfield, people talk to each other all the time and news and gossip and such are what keep folk going, half the time, know what I mean? Like, one of the Smailes lads, I can't remember which one, Stuart I think, I bumped into him and he was telling me that Snowy bought Jacob a pint in the Fox and Grape. That's a bit of news!'

Trevor almost caught himself chuckling, but Butterfield's next question came quickly, 'When was this?'

'It was after Snowy nearly killed the rabbit with his van. There was a bit of a fuss about it. The kids keep a rabbit at the school and it escaped into the road. Snowy was driving his old van through the village and stunned the thing and the kids were upset and crying and Snowy was effing and jeffing. They reckon

Jacob knew what to do, 'cos he revived the rabbit somehow. Don't ask me how he did it. Anyhow, that night, Snowy was still fuming in the pub but Jacob soon got around him and, like I say, Snowy ends up buying him a beer.'

'Hmmm, I see.'

'Then there was the time when the three of us were in the shed at Brompton and…'

'The three of you? Which three was that?'

For the first time, Trevor sensed that Butterfield probably knows the answer to his own question, 'Sorry, I thought I told you about us working in the garden together. Jacob, Fred and me.'

'That's ok. You three are quite close, then?'

'Yeah. You could say that. Don't get me wrong, I get on with the folk at the allotments, but Jacob and Fred are easy to talk to and they get stuck in, know what I mean?'

'Yep. Good workers, the salt of the Earth.'

'That's it. Anyway, we were in the shed. I think we'd had a bite to eat, and we were looking at an old picture frame that Jacob had been asked to repair for the Vicar. He made a good job of it. There was another little picture that he found and we were looking at it when Snowy poked his head in the door to see what was going on, like. I half expected him to kick off with some jibe about lazy buggers always skiving off in the shed, that sort of thing, you know? But, he didn't. He had a quick look, had a bit of a laugh with us, and went on his way. It was a bit of nothing but it stuck in my mind 'cos it wasn't like him. I don't know what to read into it. I don't even know why I'm gabbing on about it, but as we're talking and you said anything…'

'Absolutely, Trevor. Thank you for this. It might help, who knows?'

'Is that it then, Mister Butterfield? Are we done? Can I go now?'

Butterfield pushed his chair away from the desk and smiled, 'Yes, I think that's all. Oh, hang on a minute. Just a quicky.'

Trevor began to laugh, but remained seated, 'It's like the guy on the telly. Colombo. Just one more thing.'

Phil Butterfield couldn't conceal his glee and threw his head back to laugh at the ceiling, 'You got me there, Trevor. I'll take it as a compliment. Colombo. I've been called many things, but I've never been compared to him before. No, all I wanted to ask you about was your relationship with Fred and Jacob. According to Fred, you'd all had a tough day clearing away the rubbish from the shed fire into the skip and you were all tired by the time it came to going home. You went off home a bit early didn't you? Before the others. Can't say I blame you. Mucky work, back for a bath, back to the family, yes?'

'Yeah. Pretty dog tired, we'd got through a lot.'

'Except you didn't go home, did you, Trevor? You turned up after the shots were fired but you would have had to be a bloody fast cyclist to get back from your house in the time between you cycling home and then arriving on that horrendous scene in the garden. So, could you tell me what you did when you left Fred and Jacob?'

Trevor cleared his throat and folded his arms, 'Yeah. I've got nothing to hide. I just didn't think it was very important.'

'I know, I know. Like I said, this is just a chat. Every detail, no matter how small…'

'Yeah. Right. Well, I was going to go home, but I had something on my mind, so I decided to speak to Camilla about it. See, that picture I was telling you about, the one Jacob found when he repaired the picture frame, it troubled me a bit.'

'Oh? Why was that?'

'Well, it reminded me of someone I knew once. A man called Barney Sutton. Camilla knew him as well. He was a lovely little fella, used to have an allotment. The man in the picture was the spitting image of Barney in his younger days. I couldn't figure out what his picture was doing tucked behind Miss Bennett's old picture frame with the old priest. It didn't sit right in my head.'

'Miss Bennett?'

'Yes. It was her picture frame. The Vicar arranged for it to be fixed.'

'And what did Camilla Wilberforce make of all this?'

'Well, I reckon we agreed, the two of us, that it was Barney Sutton. But, we were talking about it when we heard the shots.'

'That's when the two of you ran from the house to the garden.'

'Yep.'

Butterfield pulled a handkerchief from his cardigan and wiped his nose, a look of concentration on his brow, 'You were fond of this man, Barney Sutton, the two of you, I mean?'

'Oh yes. He was a lovely fella. Sweet little guy! With his plants and herbs down at the allotment. And his amazing shed and his scarecrow. Oh, now then, there's another thing I forgot. Funny how things just pop back into your head. It was Jacob, I think, who spotted it. Camilla brought Barney's old scarecrow, Arthur, from his place to Brompton. Daft, I know, but that's how it was. But, after the shed fire, Arthur was missing. We reckon Ethel must have chucked him on the fire. Daft, eh? I forgot about that, sorry Mister Butterfield.'

'No need to be sorry. Arthur, eh? Funny name for a scarecrow. Might mean nothing at all, but you never know.'

Butterfield stood at last and extended a hand to Trevor, 'Good to meet you again, Trevor. Sorry to take you away from your work, but I am very grateful, you've been very helpful.'

CHAPTER TWENTY-EIGHT

Detective Constable Kevin Hindmarsh favoured brunettes, any day, over blondes and so was fascinated by Camilla, who was unlike anyone he had ever met; proud and from a different world, a stunner, beautiful dark eyes, long dark hair, endless legs. The first time he interviewed her, he was slightly uncomfortable, nervous even, but she took it all in her stride despite the obvious sense of shock following Ethel Elstrop's act of destruction. After the shooting of Jacob, and Snowy's apparent suicide, that all changed and Camilla suddenly resembled a startled fawn being chased by a hunting party. Strangely, she looked younger, without her usual makeup and stiletto heels, hair tied back in a ponytail; today, Camilla was a little more composed and still unbelievably attractive.

'Thanks for your time and I'm sorry to drag you through more questions but you've been extremely co-operative and we appreciate it because it helps us to piece everything together and helps to bring about some closure, hopefully, to this whole sorry business.'

He thought he got those words right. 'Closure,' usually did the trick; helped to get them opening up, just like they taught in training, 'Ok, let's see, we have your statement thanks and, like I said before, this is a completely informal follow-up, er…may I call you Camilla?'

'Actually, you didn't, but it's fine. Anything to assist, yes, you may.'

'Right. How many people do you actually employ at Brompton Hall?'

'This might sound strange, but the only two employed permanently are, were, Snowy and Ethel, and you could say I inherited them along with the property when Aunt Harriett died.'

'It's a big place to run on your own, isn't it?'

'My aunt preferred things that way, she was a strong-minded and capable woman. There are plenty of volunteers who help in the grounds, out of love for her and for the place itself. It works well, so why change it?'

'But, our understanding is that Jacob is an employee also, is that correct?'

'He is employed on a temporary basis without a contract of employment. He didn't want or need a contract, that's what he told me. I pay him in cash for whatever jobs he carries out. He's a good worker who needed some work.'

'All the same, he hasn't been around these parts very long, you must be a very trusting person?'

'You'd be surprised how trusting I can be, Detective Constable, but I'm not a complete idiot. I did my homework. This is a small village and I've learned to trust the word of those I've come to love and respect. And, sometimes, one has to trust one's own judgement, I'm sure you'll agree.'

'I see. And so far as you are aware, the Elstrops were ok with these arrangements?'

'Of course. Why wouldn't they be?'

'Perhaps they might have seen this stranger as some sort of threat, a new kid on the block who might start to take over their territory, if you see what I mean?'

'Well, that's not the case, I can assure you.'

'And Mister Sudron. Roy. Where does he fit into these arrangements?'

Camilla paused to run her fingers through her hair to her ponytail, 'Roy is a very good friend. He has been very supportive since I took over at Brompton. He's very knowledgeable on most matters to do with rural life.'

'He isn't an employee, though.'

'No.'

'It was Trevor Matthews, and you, who arrived on the scene after you heard the gunshots. Trevor is another Brompton volunteer, yes?'

'Yes.'

'How well do you know him?'

'Well, enough to trust him implicitly, if that's what you mean.'

'Yes, I'm sure. He's been very helpful. You know him pretty well, then?'

'Yes. I first came across him just after Aunt Harriet died. It was a stressful time, and I needed people to talk to. People who knew and loved her. Trevor was one of them. He has an allotment, and he also comes here occasionally to help. Another very good worker.'

Hindmarsh decided it was time to pause, thoughtfully, for effect, just as Phil Butterfield suggested, before throwing in the next question, 'Does the name Barney Sutton mean anything to you?'

Camilla's fingers went to her hair once more. Kevin noticed that she had cleared her throat. Most of them seem to do that.

'He was someone I met at the allotment. Trevor introduced me to him. It turns out that he had been a friend and confidante of my aunt. They met when both of them were receiving similar medical treatment at the hospital. Sadly, he died not long after my aunt passed away. It was rather distressing, I had grown rather fond of him. He was extremely kind and thoughtful.'

'What about Arthur?'

Camilla attempted a forced smile, but it proved less than convincing.

'That was the name he gave his scarecrow, down at the allotment. I brought it here, to be honest, to remember him by. Silly, I suppose, but there it is.'

'Trevor seems to think that Ethel Elstrop may have thrown Arthur onto the fire when she set the shed alight.'

'Yes, I know.'

'Why would she do that, do you think, Camilla?'

'I wish I knew, but I don't have a clue.'

'Did you bring anything else?'

'Sorry, I don't understand.'

'Anything else of Barney Sutton's to remember him by.'

'Yes, as a matter of fact. By your question, I assume you have spoken to Trevor and you're referring to the old file that belonged to Barney.'

'Tell me about the old file, sounds interesting.'

'It is. Barney kept a good number of them in his allotment hut. They were full of drawings of plants, beautifully drawn and painted, from his time at sea. He kept many fascinating old artifacts. That was the only thing I kept.'

'Why that file?'

'It was the one I came across after he died. It's a beautiful thing, it really is. It has drawings and paintings of the Monocot family.'

'Who are they?'

'Monocots are orchids, Detective Constable Hindmarsh.'

'So they are, Camilla. And I suspect you know also that spelt backwards, the name is TOCONOM.'

CHAPTER TWENTY-NINE

Geoffrey could count on the fingers of one hand the number of times he had stepped over the threshold of the Fox and Grape, 'I know, I know…it's a sad reflection of my ministry, but…'

'Look, darling. Just listen for a second, it's still summer, and the sun has not stopped shining, see? People are still out and about. The pub is making an effort and doing its bit. They've got food on and everyone just wants to get some sense of normality, so I say let's support them. Anyway, we're here now, so just relax and take in the experience and who knows? You might even enjoy yourself!'

Geoffrey gripped his wife's arm and smiled in submission, 'You're quite right. Actually, this beer is not bad. It's been a long time since I had a pint of draught.'

'There you are, not so bad, eh?'

Julia took another sip of her white wine spritzer and secretly congratulated herself on this mini-triumph of her own creation, having suggested to her husband that it may send out messages of community togetherness and cohesion if she accompanied him for a pub lunch alongside Peter Stephenson. Peter had jumped at the idea and suggested he bring along Judith Balfour to make up a foursome.

'Visibility is everything when it comes to leadership, especially in times of crisis, that's what you taught me, Geoff.'

'Ok ok, I surrender.'

The pub was quite busy for a mid-week lunchtime and, to Geoffrey's slight surprise and quiet pleasure, there were no murmurs of curiosity nor the turning of heads when his little entourage planted itself at one of the tables. He found it difficult to admit to himself that he always felt a curious sense of inadequacy in the presence of Sandra and Len Hewitt, though he had rarely been in their company. Especially Sandra. Geoffrey's life values and acquired wisdom were firmly embedded in his faith, but Sandra seemed to possess a form of worldly wisdom that fascinated and eluded him. Not that she could ever be labelled intellectual, neither was she particularly articulate nor conversationally engaging, yet people listened to her and valued her opinion. Perhaps, he mused, this was what Peter meant when he referred to her as a good barmaid. Sandra had the sort of listening skills that many of his priestly colleagues lacked. Yes, that was it.

Geoffrey allowed himself to reflect on this a little longer when Sandra approached to take their order, 'The soup is mushroom today and we have steak and kidney pie, ploughman's or vegetable lasagne. Or, we can make up a round of sandwiches if you prefer. Any more drinks?'

Geoffrey requested a half to top up his pint, Julia another white wine spritzer, while Peter ordered a second pint and a gin and tonic for Judith. They all plumped for soup and ploughman's.

'I wonder if we'll see the ubiquitous Detective Superintendent Butterfield or his sidekick?'

Julia held her glass to the light, 'Cheers everyone. You mean Kevin Hindmarsh, the Detective Constable?'

Peter stroked his beard and chuckles, 'Wow! That's a bit familiar, isn't it? Do you use their Christian names all the time, even when they're giving you the third degree?'

'Well, why not? Actually, I've quite warmed to Phil Butterfield, he strikes me as a kindly soul at heart, behind the tough police veneer.'

Judith, relaxing into the conversation, leaned back in her seat, her big toe nudging Peter's leg under the table; she's chosen to wear casual jeans and sweater today, Peter seemed to prefer the casual look, 'We're not supposed to use the term 'Christian' name any more at school. It's first and second names only these days.'

'How sad.'

'Has anyone heard how poor Jacob is doing? No news from the hospital?'

'I rang this morning but there's nothing new, I'm afraid. Stable and comfortable.'

'Good news, I suppose.'

Judith leaned forward again, 'I'll never forget our little episode with Oscar the rabbit. Jacob is the school hero. Jimmy Thompson's parents have agreed to look after Oscar over the summer holidays, I think they are used to keeping lots of pets in their back yard. I only hope the poor little thing survives the six weeks break. It doesn't bear thinking about if anything should go wrong.'

'Perish the thought. Hilda would be inconsolable.'

'Not to mention…uncontrollable.'

'And what about Ethel? What on earth is going on? I drove past the Elstrop house this morning and most of the reporters have gone for now, but there were still a couple of them hanging around. I gather she's just holed herself up. Even Butterfield can't get a squeak out of her. Why doesn't she take a break, go to stay with family or friends? Camilla doesn't want her prosecuted for the shed fire, that much I know because she told me so. She just wants to understand why?'

'Don't we all?'

A tall girl wearing huge earrings, multi-coloured fingernails and a tattoo on each wrist, emerged from the kitchen, carrying two large plates towards their table. Geoffrey thought he could remember her in a girl guide uniform, but could not bring her name to mind.

'Four ploughman's. Sorry, I can only manage two at a time.'

Julia cleared a space on the table and the girl, carefully and slowly, placed the plates before her and Judith.

'Hi Sophie. Is this your summer job, working in the pub?'

Yep. Saving up for college.'

'Good for you, what are you going to study?'

'Forensics. If I get my grades…and I will get them. By the way, Oscar the rabbit is fine. Our Brian goes next door to the Thompsons every night just to make sure. I heard you talking while I was serving those folks at the next table.'

'That's good to know.'

'I'll just fetch the other two ploughman's.'

'Don't want them to get cold…joke.'

A small hush descended as their meals were served, when Sophie was finally out of sight behind the kitchen door, the eating began and the conversation resumed.

'Better tell Butterfield about young Sophie there, she'll make a brilliant detective one day, keeps her ear close to the ground, that one!'

Geoffrey paused to look Peter in the eye, 'Speaking of keeping one's ear to the ground. What are the pub regulars saying? Any theories?'

'Well, Judith and I popped in last evening just for half an hour, people are still trying to get their heads around the whole business. The place won't be the same without Snowy, that's for sure. Love him or loathe him, he was a character. There's a real sense of shock and bewilderment, but no one can understand why it happened the way it did. No one.'

'Yes, of course. One wouldn't expect anything else. It's so difficult to comprehend. I think…'

Geoffrey's phone, shoved deep inside his favoured sports jacket, was unmistakable.

'Ignore it, darling, we're having a break. If it's urgent, they'll ring back.'

'Yes, ok.'

His face a mask of apprehension and doubt, he removed his phone, pressed the red button to stop the call and placed it on the table next to his glass, but it would not be denied and, this time, he answered, 'Hello there…yes…how can I help? I see…well, I suppose…tomorrow morning then…yes…I'll be ready…fine…yes…bye.'

Julia folded her arms and waited for her husband to explain the nature of the call while the others kept a respectful silence.

'That was Phil Butterfield. He wants to speak to Marcia Bennett.'

'Miss Bennett, why on earth…'

'I don't know, but he wants me to accompany him, tomorrow morning.'

CHAPTER THIRTY

Phil Butterfield gave up smoking twenty years ago, but a day never passed without, at some point, the familiar craving for the comfort of his pipe. The vicar was an amiable enough chap, but he was an innocent, a sheep, an academic who probably believed that if you could gather enough information and data on any issue under the sun, then you could solve any problem. If only.

'Jacob is awake and talking and walking, I just got word from the hospital.'

Phil was made to read a lot of management and leadership guff at various times in his career, most of it written by academics who couldn't manage a booze up in a brewery. There was one paper, however, that still stuck in his mind and he was thinking of it now, as he squatted next to Geoffrey in the rear seats of the police car, staring blankly at the back of Kevin Hindmarsh's head. The author of the paper explained the necessity of understanding the politics of leadership and management and gave examples of four distinct and important character or personality traits. These traits could, in a sense, define a person as an ox, or a sheep, or a wolf, or an owl. Kevin was currently behaving like a workmanlike ox, but had the potential to become an owl with the right people to support him. Geoffrey was a sheep and always would be, bless him.

A small bird flew past the car window and briefly interrupted his thoughts before he could re-focus, 'You and I both have jobs where we have to come face to face with the idea of good and evil, would you agree Geoffrey? May I call you Geoffrey?'

'Geoff. Yes, I understand what you mean, Detective Superintendent, though we operate, for want of a better expression, in different ways; perhaps, in many aspects, to achieve a similar aim: the triumph of one over the other, good over evil.'

'Call me Phil. Hmm. When I look back now, I can think of many occasions when I have known, for certain, that I was in the presence of evil, as if I could smell evil on the breath or the clothes of some individual that I had to arrest or interrogate. It might be in their voice, or their eyes or something in their movements, but, whatever, it is an unmistakable stench.'

'We all possess different skills and talents, thank God. The important thing is that we use them wisely for the greater good. There are those within the church who are very skilled in exorcisms, for example, though that has never been an aspect of my own ministry.'

'But, you're not saying that you wouldn't recognise true evil if you were confronted by it?'

'Let me answer that by asking you a similar question. Is there a danger in your line of work that you become so hardened and desensitised that you find it difficult to recognise true goodness when you see it?'

Butterfield was suddenly animated and leaned forward to tap Kevin Hindmarsh on the shoulder, the car pulled in to a layby.

'You see that's it, Geoff! That's exactly what it is! We've been interviewing folk around Clamford for hours on end, asking all the right questions, interviewing witnesses, gathering all the pieces together. What do we have? We have a series of events:

an act of arson, a violent attempt on a man's life, and an equally violent suicide. Terrible deeds committed in an otherwise respectable and peaceful village, and yet I sense not a whiff of evil anywhere. Ok, Snowy Elstrop could be a nasty piece of work when he'd had a drink but…evil? Nah. I've met rapists, child molesters, murderers, and I know the smell of evil. So, after all these years, are my senses weakening?'

'I doubt that, very much.'

'And you are right to doubt that. The answers don't lie in the raw data, the stark witness statements or the bald evidence. The answers lie beneath and behind those things, in places where most people wouldn't think to look. Sometimes, life and circumstances combine, somehow, to make decent people do indecent and evil things. I don't understand why that happens the way it does, Geoff, maybe you do. But, it's my job to find out how they happen and to apply that know-how to this case. See what I mean?'

Kevin twisted around in the driver's seat, 'Sir, I've got another message. Jacob is fit enough to talk.'

'Good, good. You drop us off at the Care Home, then get yourself over to the hospital. And now I would very much appreciate it if you, Geoff, would be kind enough to tell me everything you know about Miss Marcia Bennett.'

The day was dry but a little overcast as the car negotiated the narrow lanes through the Vale of Clamford towards the outskirts of Larchester and the grounds of Ramsden House. In the car park of the Care Home, Geoffrey sighed as he caught a glimpse of Marcia's white hair at the window of her room.

'I feel that I've rather betrayed a trust. She's a dear lady and I have no wish to hurt her feelings. Only my curate, Peter Stephenson, and I know about her history, the unwanted pregnancy and...'

'So far as you are aware, you are the only ones who know the story, that's what you mean isn't it?'

'Well yes, of course.'

'Of course. Shall we go in? See you later, Detective Constable.'

The car edged away up the drive. As it picked up speed and disappeared through the trees, the weary world watchers at the entrance door sat, impassive and expressionless in their wheelchairs to stare at it.

The two men followed the customary ritual of signing in the visitors' book and cleansing the hands with ant-bacterial lotion from a small dispenser, just at the moment Jane Simpson emerged from her office.

'Good morning, gentlemen. You've come to see Marcia?'

'Good morning Jane, this is Detective Superintendent Butterfield. Yes, we've come this morning because he would like to speak to her about one or two things connected with the investigation he's leading. He's asked me along so that...'

Butterfield stepped forward, and Jane felt her slim hand fully encased in his warm grip, 'I'm very pleased to meet you Jane, may I call you Jane? Yes, I've invited Geoff along so that Miss Bennett has a friendly face to support her, the last thing I want to do is to cause her any unnecessary discomfort or distress. I'm afraid, it's in the nature of my work to ask a lot of questions of people who rarely, if ever, come face-to-face with police officers.'

'Of course, I understand. You have an important job to do Mister Butterfield, such a dreadful thing to happen in Clamford.'

'Please call me Phil and thank you for your understanding. You too have an important job here and you seem to do it very well, from what I hear.'

Jane's hand was gently released, 'Well, thank you. We are a team here at Ramsden House and it's my role to make sure we all maintain the highest standards of care for our residents.'

'Absolutely, that's quite a weight of responsibility for one so young, if I may say so. When you reach my age, you rely heavily on the value of years of experience, but I can easily recall the challenges of my early career. It was a steep learning curve, believe me. You have my admiration and respect, Jane.'

'Thank you, it is a challenge but I enjoy my work here, it's very rewarding.'

'Good, good, that's the spirit. So, down to business…how is Miss Bennett today, after her fall?'

'Oh, she seems in good spirits. She polished off her breakfast and she's managing her walking stick a lot better as each day passes.'

'Ah, that's good to hear. Remind me, Jane, how did it happen? How did she fall?'

'We're not entirely sure, but it seems she might have got up out of her chair too quickly and felt a little dizzy. She took a step and knocked her knee against a low table and down she went. It can happen, of course, with the elderly. Our residents enjoy as much independence and privacy as we can safely provide and that means that my staff aren't with them every hour of the day, on an individual basis. Marcia sometimes joins in with the others in the residents' lounge and for meals but, she also seems to enjoy her own company in her room.'

'Of course, I understand…and how soon was someone able to come to her aid?'

'Almost straight away. She was clearly in pain, but, to be honest, she was very brave. She seemed more upset about the damage to her things than her injuries.'

'Yes, I see. You mean the photograph frame?'

Jane nodded and beamed at Geoffrey, 'I'm very grateful you managed to get it repaired so quickly. You have no idea how that pleased her.'

'I can imagine. Well, thank you Jane, it was a pleasure to meet you, may we pop along to Marcia's room now?'

'Yes, of course. I'll arrange for someone to bring some refreshments.'

They walked in single file along the corridor, Geoffrey with his eyes fixed on the laminated flooring while Phil Butterfield held his head high and alert, a good two yards behind.

Geoffrey tapped lightly on Marcia's door and opened it.

'Good morning, Geoffrey, do come in. Good morning, Detective Superintendent, I've been expecting you. Please sit down, I asked one of the staff to bring a couple of comfy seats as I am not sure how long you envisage this may take. I expect someone will bring refreshments in a minute or two, they're very good like that.'

'It's a pleasure to meet you, Miss Bennett, may I call you Marcia? My name's Phil, by the way.'

'Yes, I know and yes you may.'

Butterfield was instantly warming to this lady, so full of elegance with a subtle hint of dry wit, it was turning out to be a most rewarding morning.

'You've been a stranger to Clamford these past few years, Philip, but some of we oldies remember times past with great clarity. I recall the Barnett murder enquiry which you led, in Larchester, must be all of twenty-five years ago, I suppose. It was quite exciting to see so many police officers in the village. A fascinating case, I followed it closely. I remember it well, I have a good memory, always had. Still got all my marbles even if this old body of mine is not as fit as it used to be.'

She chuckled gently to herself, her eyes dancing from one man to the other.

'That was a difficult case, Marcia, and it was a real challenge to get all the evidence together so that we could be sure of a prosecution. People were reluctant to come forward, but we got there in the end.'

'Yes, you did. It was a most upsetting case.'

'Indeed. This latest business is a very different cup of tea but, in a funny old way, just as difficult, and just as upsetting. We know what happened, of course, we know the protagonists, but we don't have a motive. That's what makes it so upsetting. What in God's name possessed the Elstrops to do what they did?'

'Well, whatever was done was not done in God's name, Philip. Ah, here's the tea.'

Geoffrey couldn't conceal his surprise that it was Jane who delivered the refreshments, 'I hope we're not putting you to any trouble, Jane.'

'Not at all. If there's anything else we can help you with, just ask.'

Then she slipped away into the laminated corridors. Marcia leaned forward, her voice hushed, 'I had hoped that, perhaps, Jane and your curate, Peter, might have made a good couple but, I fear, that ship may have sailed. Am I correct, Geoffrey?'

'I think there is little that escapes your attention.'

'Quite so.'

The tea was strong, the way Marcia liked it, and the biscuits were chocolate covered, which suited Butterfield just fine.

'So…now…down to business. I expect, Philip, that Geoffrey has appraised you of my background story, am I correct?'

Startled for a second, Geoffrey wiped away a few drops of tea that fell on his trousers, 'I am so sorry if that offends you, my dear, but I felt compelled to divulge what you told Peter and I in confidence, in the interests of assisting the police, you understand?'

'I would expect no less of you, Geoffrey. I would have done the same in your position. You are forgiven. Now, what is it you wish to discuss, Mister Butterfield…Philip?'

'Well, thank you for being so candid, Marcia. I see you now have both of your photographs in their frames. Do you have any more?'

'None. I keep scrap books but they are solely collections of memorabilia, mainly to do with the village and the Clamford Vale. Magazine articles and old maps. I'm not one for photograph collections. My family is locked away in the past, in my memory vaults, I'm afraid. That's where I prefer to keep them.'

'I see. That strikes me as rather sad.'

'I'm not a sad person, no, I tend to be pragmatic about things and Clamford has been good to me over the years. I carved out a pleasant little life among people I became very fond of.'

Butterfield eased himself up from his armchair to examine the photograph of the old priest, 'Henry Cattermole, he was quite a character in Larchester.'

'You remember him?'

'Before my time, but I still hear some people refer to him occasionally. Part of my job is to get to know local names, from the present and the past.'

'I think of him as a friend and ally, someone who stood up for me when I needed support and comfort.'

'It was Henry who made all the arrangements for your child to be sent away for adoption?'

'That's right, he pacified my parents, especially my father, and poured oil on troubled waters. I think of him often, he died in the early seventies, I saw the newspaper obituary.'

Butterfield turned his attention to the other photograph of the jovial young sailor, 'You've had this one framed, I see.'

'Jane brought me the frame, it belonged to one of the residents who no longer wanted it. Very kind of her. Now, he has a place next to dear Henry.'

'Remind me about how you acquired this picture.'

'It was pushed through my door, in a plain envelope, I never discovered who sent it.'

'But you knew who was in the picture, straight away?'

'Immediately. My child, all grown up in his uniform. The smile, the eyes, everything.'

'Could it have been Henry Cattermole who delivered it to your door?'

'That notion did cross my mind, but who knows?'

'Do you mind if I remove it from the frame for a second, just a second? I promise to put it back together.'

'If you must, but I can tell you what you'll find...the letters B and S. That's all. Before you ask the obvious, no, I have no idea what the initials stand for.'

'And the father of your child, you never saw him again?'

'I had no wish to see him and no desire to track him down.'

'His name was Arthur, is that correct?'

'Correct.'

'Hmmm. Interesting.'

'Is it? How?'

Philip Butterfield replaced the little photograph in its proper position and settled back in the armchair, his fingers gently tapping out a rhythm on his right knee, his eyes fixed on some point in the far distance of his memory, 'Marcia, have you come across a man called Trevor Matthews?'

'I don't think so, unless you mean the chap they call Tattoo Trevor. Is that the chap?'

'That's him. Know him?'

'Not really. I know of him. Seems a nice man. People speak very well of him. I used to see him around the village, not often, he always nodded and smiled. But, no, can't say I know him, really. Why do you ask?'

'How well do you know Camilla Wilberforce?'

'Everyone knows Camilla. Of course, her aunt Harriet and I were close, so I was very aware of Camilla before she came to Clamford on a permanent basis. Harriet and I enjoyed each other's company, she was a delight. I miss her. Of course, living here at Ramside, I've lost touch with many people. I used to enjoy going to Brompton House, walking around the gardens with Harriet. Camilla put on a rather splendid garden party in the grounds after Harriett's service of remembrance. It was quite an occasion, wasn't it Geoffrey?'

'It certainly was. No expense spared.'

'Just about everyone was there: the Sudrons, the Elstrops, the Pearsons, the Smailes…everyone.'

'But you don't know Camilla very well?'

'No, I don't, I'm afraid.'

'I see. Well, I think we've covered everything. Thank you for your time, Marcia. You've been most helpful.'

'I can't imagine how that's possible. I haven't told you anything, really.'

'No, No…it's been very useful. There's just one last question.'

Marcia's eyes twinkled with delight, 'There always is, I love a good detective mystery.'

Butterfield took it on the chin, 'You're one step ahead of me. I've been sussed.'

'So, ask me the killer question.'

'Does the name Barney Sutton mean anything to you?'

Marcia tipped her head to one side as a frown of concentration covered her brow until the colour began to fade, quickly, from her cheeks. Butterfield watched as her gaze switched to the little photograph of the sailor.

'Barney Sutton. I don't know anyone with that name. Who is he, Philip? Oh, wait...no. I see. The initials B and S. Are you telling me that B and S stand for, no, I don't understand.'

'I'm not telling you anything, my dear, I just asking, that's all.'

CHAPTER THIRTY-ONE

Ted Smailes cared little for hospitals. He always told Doris that it was the smell of disinfectant and antiseptic that put him off visiting, but the truth was they made him feel afraid. Of course, Doris knew this and said nothing. Another truth was that, until last year's heart attack, he had rarely suffered a day's illness in his life. Above all things that life offered, what Ted loved most was fresh air: the feel of it on the skin, the rawness of it against his cheeks on a fresh January day or the softness of it when an unexpected breeze of August warmth carried the scent of grass across the meadow. So, his spirits were lifted when a staff nurse invited him to wait in the octangle-shaped garden of Larchester General Hospital where small bench seats were shaded by cherry blossom trees, cypress and leylandii.

'The doctor is with him now, I'm sure he won't be long.'

'How is he doing?'

'You'll see for yourself. He's doing fine.'

The bright sun was not long past its meridian. Ted removed his jacket, loosened his shirt collar and settled back beneath a cherry blossom tree to check his phone; no messages, everything was fine on the farm, the boys had it all in hand. It would have been very easy to surrender to sleep in this little garden. Maybe he should have brought a newspaper from Millers shop. Then again, it' had been a long time since he bothered to read a paper, or a magazine for that matter.

A chaffinch hopped onto an overhanging branch on the other side of the garden, experimented with its tail feathers for a second or two then, as abruptly as it arrived, scooted away above the hospital roof tops.

Not that Ted missed his old life, when his days were filled by endless jobs around the farm, quarrelling with Doris, making up with Doris, joining in with the lads down at the Fox and Grape, dreaming up new ways to raise more cash for some new beasts. They were good days, but he wouldn't want to go back to them, not anymore. Now, he had time to think, time to look, really look…at everything and anything. He didn't know what to think about next.

He felt nervous, but why should that be? Ted tried to figure this out, under the tree. He'd seen illness before. There was the time Stuart fell off the tractor seat and broke his arm; or when Doris nearly cut her finger off with a kitchen knife and there was blood all over the place. It' was just that illness and injury didn't sit comfortably on a man like Jacob, they didn't belong on a man like that. They' were cruel intruders. It' was not the same around Clamford when Jacob's was not around. He could recall every word Jacob had said to him, just about, but he couldn't bring to mind what Doris talked about over breakfast. Silly bugger, it was only a couple of weeks since he turned up on that old horse, and he'd probably scarper as far away as he could when he felt up to it. Who could blame him…getting shot like that? Made no sense to stick around here. But, he would be missed alright, that's for sure.

A door slid open and a young man stepped out into the garden, Ted recognised him at once, Detective Constable Kevin Hindmarsh had become a very familiar figure in Clamford.

'Hello there, Mister Smailes. May I join you?'

Though there was plenty of room on the bench, Ted shuffled along, instinctively.

'Aye lad. Another grand day, eh? What are you doing here?'

'I expect you already know, don't you? We got a message to say Jacob is recovering well, walking and talking.'

'It's good news at last, isn't it? He's a good'un is Jacob.'

'You're not the first person to tell me that. He hasn't been in Clamford long mind you, has he?'

'Doesn't take long with some folk. You can tell the cut of his jib straight away.'

'He's a tenant in your cottage, isn't he? The cottage you bought from Miss Bennett.'

'Well, I suppose he is, but, to be honest, I think of him more as a pal.'

The chaffinch returned to the tree and, on this occasion, it stuck around long enough to watch the sliding door open once more and a young nurse step through with Jacob. He was dressed in his customary tee shirt and jeans and was walking unaided, but a little slower than usual. When he spied Ted and Kevin Hindmarsh, he smiled and waves for a second before walking over to their bench seat and extending his hand to both men.

The young nurse made sure he was seated comfortably before stepping back, 'I'll leave you to speak to the officer but please don't tire yourself out too much. When you've had enough, come back inside, Jacob.'

The chaffinch flitted to the end of the branch for a closer look, then flew off into the sky.

'You don't have to worry about me, I'm fine. It's good to be outside.'

Kevin Hindmarsh was about to introduce himself, but Ted was not to be denied, 'I came yesterday and the day before but you weren't properly awake. It's good to see you looking so well. Wait 'till I tell Doris and the boys. And before you ask, Joey's just fine, he's eating well and his coat is looking good. We take him for a trot and a graze on the meadow every morning. You'll be chuffed to bits at how well he's looking, his eyes are bright and alert.'

'I'm really grateful to you. Tell Doris thank you and I'll be back to see Joey very soon.'

'I'll tell her, she'll be pleased, everyone will be happy. Well, I'll pop back to see you when you've finished with the officer. They do a nice sandwich in the visitor's area. See you later.'

Jacob turned to Hindmarsh who was feeling slightly wrong-footed. Keen to regain some control over the situation, he invited Jacob to sit down next to him, under the shade.

Silence descended on the garden for a full minute.

'I am Detective Constable Kevin Hindmarsh and I need to ask you a few questions as part of our enquiry into the incidents at Brompton Hall when you were injured. Nothing to worry about. We just want to establish the facts about what happened and what led up to the events of that day. That's all, ok?'

Jacob nodded and smiled, but said nothing.

'Tell me, who are you?'

'Hasn't anyone told you?'

'Your name.'

'Jacob.'

'Yes, that's the name on your bed and that's what everyone calls you, but that's all we have. Jacob. That's all.'

'I have no connections around here. I come from somewhere further afield.'

This time, it was Hindmarsh's turn to nod, 'Right. Fair enough. So, what's your full name?'

'Jacob Robson.'

Hindmarsh took out a small notebook and began to write, 'And where do you come from?'

'Well, at the moment I'm living in Clamford, in Ted Smailes's cottage.'

'Originally, where do you come from… originally?'

'I was born in Stockton, but my parents moved around a lot when I was a nipper. I take after them.'

'So, you don't have a fixed, permanent address?'

'Nope.'

'But you keep a horse. You ride. Are you a traveller, then?'

'We're all travellers, aren't we? Look, let me make it easier for you. I go where I want to go and I find work where I can.'

'Ok I see. And you found work at Brompton Hall?'

'Yep.'

'What sort of work?'

'At first it was just voluntary but then, when they saw that I was keen and could put a decent shift in, well Camilla took me on proper. Started off with heavy gardening work, digging and weeding, cleaning out the greenhouses, shifting all the unwanted rubbish. Then I started on the shed, tidying it all up, sorting out the good stuff from the bad. There was plenty to keep me busy. I enjoy it, they're a decent crowd of folk, volunteers and such.'

'And you formed friendships with Trevor Matthews and Mister Pickles in particular, that's right, isn't it?'

'Right enough, yeah. Pickles, is it? I never asked Fred what his name is, or Trevor, for that matter, never seemed to be important.'

'Snowy Elstrop was the headman, around the grounds. How did that work out?'

'Headman? I suppose that's how he saw himself. Him and his missus were on the payroll, but it's Camilla and Roy who pull all the strings. That's how I see it, anyhow. Isn't any of my business, I just get on with whatever they want me to get on with and the rest takes care of itself.'

'How did you get on with him?'

'You mean Roy…or Snowy?'

Kevin Hindmarsh looked harder into the eyes of this curious man. They were warm and friendly, the face open and devoid of any malice or mistrust; he answered the questions with no hint of hesitation. There was a beguiling authority about the way he spoke, yet he seemed non-judgemental, almost gentle despite his undoubted strength and vigour. This interview should have been easy enough and straightforward, and in an obvious sense it was…so why did he have the nagging feeling that he was getting out of his depth?

He pretended to write a few more notes in his little book to play for time and gather his thoughts, 'I mean Snowy, how did you get on with him?'

'I never had a problem with Snowy.'

'That's not what I asked.'

Jacob spied the chaffinch in a high branch and watched it hopping about for a few moments, 'Then ask me what you really want to know. Why did Snowy shoot me in the chest?'

'I'm listening.'

'Aye lad. They all listen, but they don't all hear. Why do folk commit acts like that, do you think? Is it out of hate, or revenge or what? I'll tell you why...because they're afraid. Hate and revenge, resentment and the like, they all come out of fear.'

'Are you telling me that Snowy Elstrop was afraid of you? Why was that?'

'That's where you've got me. I haven't a clue.'

Hindmarsh paused for effect, it was time to add some gravity to the questioning, 'Are you telling me the truth, Jacob?'

'It's the only language I know. Why would I bother to lie? He must have had his reasons, but I don't know what he was thinking when he pulled the trigger. But, I know it must have something to do with fear.'

Hindmarsh was about to try another tack when his mobile phone came to life, it was Phil Butterfield.

'Sir...yes...yes...not yet...ok...I'll let you know...bye.'

Jacob scanned the sky, but the chaffinch had flown.

'Sorry about that, Jacob. It was my boss, I'll have to get back so I won't keep you any longer and I'm very pleased to see that you are recovering well.'

'Thank you. I hope to be getting back to the village soon, when they sign me out of here. I want to see Joey my horse and the folks at Clamford.'

'Of course you do. Just a couple more quick questions, if I may…does the word Toconom mean anything to you?'

Jacob smiled, 'Just a word, that's all.'

'And does the name Barney Sutton mean anything to you?'

For the first time that day, Jacob's face was drained of colour.

CHAPTER THIRTY-TWO

Phil Butterfield watched the flashes of light sparkle from the rippled rings of water as they flowed outwards towards the banks of the river beneath the metal bridge. He only had two pebbles left in his left palm. The next shot hit a small rock with a sharp crack and then bounced away in silence, but the final throw made a resounding, satisfying plop as it nosedived into the still waters closest to the mossy bank. A small bird with dark spots on its plumage flitted away, off towards the sheep meadow and the hills beyond.

'Do you remember that day, Kevin, when they unveiled Harriet Wilberforce's statue? I was on a case on the other side of Larchester and you were…'

'I was just finishing the training course.'

'Yes. Anyway. You and I weren't here when that took place, but everybody on the Force knew what was going on, 'cos of all the fuss being made by the press people and the locals. All over a bloody statue. Split the village in two. Looking back now, it was a lot of fuss over nowt but all the same, feelings ran high in these parts. Folk scattered off carrying their own little burdens of anger and resentment…'

'I remember it happening, Sir.'

'Then it settled down again and this here bridge we're standing on, and that statue over there, they became symbols of hope and recovery for Clamford. Things turned for the better and folk were reunited with each other.'

'Very philosophical, Boss.'

Butterfield laughed and slapped his young colleague on the shoulder, 'Hoy! Watch it. All I'm saying is that a wise copper always has to know which way the wind is blowing, see what I mean? What are people feeling right now? Are the ripples flowing out somewhere and scattering the birds away...or are they slowing down, calmer, bringing everything back to where it was? Tell me again. You did exactly as I asked?'

'Yes, Sir. Exactly. I asked him if the name Barney Sutton meant anything to him.'

'And there was a reaction?'

'He looked shaken, but he said nothing.'

'Then you left?'

'Yes, I left.'

'Good, good.'

'The nurse came out to fetch him back to the ward, I got in the car and met you, we dropped the vicar off at the church and came here.'

'Right. You did well. Sometimes, you have to time these things just right. Leave questions hanging in the air. A bit like landing a fish in the stream, you won't catch the thing unless you use some bait.'

Hindmarsh grabbed the bridge handrail and began some stretching exercises by bending at the knees to lower his body down and back up, several times. Only when he'd finished could he bring himself to ask his question, 'Sorry Boss, but the thing I'm not getting is why you didn't want me to carry on questioning him. He was ready to tell us more, I know it.'

'Yep. You're right, he was ready, he would probably have told us something about this Barney Sutton that might help us. Then again, he was tired and it might have been stuff we already knew. The point is, he will still be ready to talk because he's primed now, he'll go for the bait if we play it right.'

'Yeah, but even so…'

'Look at what we've got: bits and pieces from all the folk we've interviewed and questioned and chatted to with one central character in the middle of all those scattered fragments. Barney Sutton. Who was he and what's the link with the attack on Jacob and Snowy's suicide? The answer is floating about somewhere in the stream where all those bits are separate flotsam. We need to bring all those bits and pieces together, like switching the ripples in the river into reverse. That way, we'll be able to fit them all back together, like a jigsaw.'

'Right, Sir. I like the use of the mixed metaphors.'

'I told you…watch it!'

'No, I get it. You mean we get several witnesses in the same room at the same time and get them to talk?'

'Precisely that. Well done, Kevin. It will be like gravity, like a magnetic force, you'll see, and it will attract the one piece of jigsaw that's eluded us so far...Ethel Elstrop'

CHAPTER THIRTY-THREE

By mid-morning, the private lounge at Brompton Hall was warm and suffocating from the high sun and a heady mix of confusion and nervous anticipation, despite the comforting presence of Geoffrey Roper. The sash window squeaked as he let in some air, looking out onto the gardens below, wondering how it ever came to this. Extra seats and a few small tables had been brought from the dining room.

Roy Sudron was talking to the others, but the words were floating somewhere near the ceiling, and Geoffrey couldn't quite persuade them to settle and fall comfortably to his ears.

'It took a while to persuade her, but she's on her way now, with Camilla. We went to see her last night, Camilla and me. Ethel didn't want to know at first but Camilla stood her ground, she wouldn't give in and, eventually, the old girl opened the door to us. Turns out our timing couldn't have been better, another half hour and she'd have disappeared again. Apparently, she's been staying at a hostel type place and came back to the house to collect a few things. She's in a bit of a state, not a bit like the old Ethel.'

'How on Earth did Camilla manage to persuade her?'

Geoffrey was alert once more.

'Well, I only caught some of it, but she played it just right, she just told her the truth, told her that there will always be a place for her here, despite everything that's happened. Things can be replaced and put right, but she needs to get things out, to tell her story so that we can get some sort of closure and move on. You know what I mean, that was the gist of it, anyway.'

Trevor and Fred nodded in unison. Jacob was expressionless.

Meanwhile, Philip Butterfield and Kevin Hindmarsh were conspiring somewhere outside on the landing, their voices barely audible, waiting for the two women.

Only Marcia Bennett was smiling, blind to any tension; it was a distant, vague sort of smile, she knew that Geoffrey was looking at her again, concern was etched on his brow.

Everyone's had enough, thought Geoffrey. Please Lord, let this morning's proceedings signal the beginning of the end of this madness, let there be peace once more. He had long been aware that the consequences of a person's past actions were constantly fascinating and riveting, and so he had taught himself to view the present with a forward-looking eye. But at this precise moment, he was not inclined to do so.

Every head moved when the soft clump of the front door echoed through the walls of Brompton House.

'They're here.'

Philip Butterfield was first to catch a glimpse of Ethel's chalk-white face, hot and sick with shame and fear, as she clung to the arm of Camilla who was whispering words of encouragement.

A cloak of silence floated down like a shroud over the house. The only sound Kevin Hindmarsh could hear was from his boss who was breathing out heavily through his nostrils as the two women slowly ascended the staircase to the landing.

'Good morning, ladies. How are you, Mrs Elstrop?'

Butterfield leaned in slightly, Camilla was wearing expensive perfume, Ethel remained silent, 'Whenever you feel ready, we will begin. The others are waiting in the lounge, there's really nothing at all to fear, you know why we're here so the sooner we get this done the better for all of us, especially yourself. Okay?'

Whether it was the calm insistence of Butterfield's voice, or the slow, loosening release of Camilla's hand on her arm, but in this moment, Ethel nodded again and straightened up, her jaw set and her eyes fixed on the door to the lounge, 'I'm ready, let's get on with it.'

Kevin Hindmarsh didn't wait to be told, stepping forward to open the door. Slowly, they entered.

'Hello Ethel, come in.'

From the far side of the room, by the window, Geoffrey's voice carried warmth and not a shred of surprise.

Through the thin material of Ethel's cardigan, Butterfield could sense a slight tremble as he guided her gently towards a seat next to the fireplace. Her eyes flicked about to take in the scene: the familiar faces of Roy, Trevor and that quiet little man called Fred who lost his wife a few years back and always seemed nervous, and the Vicar over there, always fretting about something but a nice enough man. Her gaze glided now from one side of the room to the other until it rested, just for a second or two, upon Marcia Bennett and on to Jacob. Camilla took the adjacent seat. No one spoke until Kevin Hindmarsh's phone rang out.

'Not now…yes…all in hand…I'll call you.'

The sound of his voice made it real to Ethel. They were waiting and she would not disappoint them, not after she'd come this far. She turned to Camilla, 'This carpet will want a good clean after all these boots and shoes have trod all over it.'

Camilla smiled and patted her wrist.

Butterfield knelt down in front of Ethel's chair and whispered something, then retreated to the window, next to Geoffrey. Ethel gave a little cough and began her story.

'Well now, the first thing I want to say is that I'm sorry, dead sorry, for all the fuss and carry on that's been caused. I wish it had never happened, but it did, and so here we are. There now. If you'll just hear me out, you might understand. Some in this room will understand a lot better than t'others but no matter.'

'Take your time, Ethel, no rush.'

'Right, well, where to start. Before Snowy and me got married, I was just plain Ethel Sutton. My family, well most of it, has lived in these parts for generations. When I was a little lass, my grandmother used to sit me on her knee and tell me about the old times when the Suttons had land and a farm, well fixed they were. Somehow, things turned bad, and they fell on hard times. I was born at the end of the war and I never knew much of anything except Clamford and the little school and the church and, by and large, I was a happy little lass. My mother would take us to Larchester, rarely, once in a while, but we were pretty poor, really. She was a good woman, my mother, anyone will tell you that. My father was a different kettle of fish, but to me he was just…my dad. I never knew how he led her a dance, I was just a kid. He was a good-looking man, and he knew it. I was glad he was my dad…back then. It all changed when I was about twelve. Everything changed.'

Ethel turned her gaze back to Marcia who remained expressionless but for that curious smile.

'Like I say, everything changed. My father's name was Arthur. He was a bit of a dresser, liked his suits and his shoes. I idolised him for being like that. People looked at him all the time. That made me feel so good. That was my dad. How was I to know what was going on?'

'You weren't to know, Ethel. How could you? You were just a little girl who worshipped her father.'

Marcia's voice seemed to come from another place, another world, even. She sat tall in her chair, dignified, authoritative, still, confident yet fatalistic.

Butterfield stepped away from the window, 'Remind me again, Marcia, how old were you when you met Arthur?'

'Philip, you and I understand each other well enough to agree that there is no way you require a reminder, but in the interests of transparency and to get these proceedings over for everyone as soon as possible, I'll go along with your little pretence.'

Butterfield's smile was one of respect and admiration, 'And I am most grateful, Marcia.'

'I was a very young sixteen, naïve and ready to discover myself. I met him at a local dance in Larchester, an event that a friend had invited me to. It seemed very exciting as I had never been to a dance before, let alone met anyone like Arthur Sutton. It was another world.'

'You fell in love with him.'

'I did. We met a few times, always in secret to make it more exciting, knowing my parents would disapprove. I learned quickly how to tell lies, I'm ashamed to admit. I was infatuated with him, you see.'

'And you became pregnant.'

'Yes.'

'And Arthur wasn't happy about that, was he?'

'I really couldn't say whether or not he was happy. That's the sad truth of it. I confided in my mother as soon as it was clear something wasn't right. When my condition was confirmed, she informed my father and…suddenly… Arthur disappeared from my life. My pregnancy was the most miserable experience, I was very frightened indeed. It was Henry Cattermole who turned out to be my protector, if you can call him that. He arranged for me to be squirrelled away to the Midlands where I gave birth to my son. I held the baby for a few moments, but then…he was taken away. I don't think I need to elaborate at this point, do I?'

Marcia's head dropped for the first time and did not lift even when Jacob's large hand reached over to cover her own.

'And you had no idea what became of the child?'

'None.'

'Weren't you ever curious? Didn't you want to find Arthur and confront him?'

'Yes, and no. Of course, I was beyond curious. But, you must remember I was very young and very naïve…hopelessly so, in hindsight. And I was terribly lost and frightened. It was a different age, you see, with different moral standards and different ways of dealing with things. I thought I might have discovered more from the Reverend Cattermole, but no, he moved on to different places and I, somehow, persuaded myself that it would be best to move on with my life. So that's what I did. I can tell you this much with complete confidence: there has never been a day of my life when I haven't wondered what became of my child. Never a day. As for his father, Arthur, well, I simply felt betrayed, foolish and very, very angry. It was the anger which wore me down, it threatened to consume me and, I don't really understand this myself, but I knew that, somehow, I must not let this event define my life, define me. Eventually, I resolved to move on, in my own way, to carve out a new life for myself. I would do it on my own, here in Clamford. So, the answer to your second question is no. I never wanted to see Arthur again, not ever, I wanted nothing to do with him.'

Butterfield turned back to Ethel, 'And your feelings at the time? You were a young girl, but you knew that your life would not be the same, didn't you?'

'Well, he just buggered off you see. That was the cruelty of it. He disappeared from my life, the father I adored. And the family was thrown upside down, all of us. Everything I knew and loved was ruined. Shame fell on us. Even at that young age, I could recognise it. People who used to come to the house stopped coming. We weren't invited to places that we used to go to. There were all those funny looks and awkward silences.

That's when I started to hate him. I hated most people when I was young and growing up, after what happened. There was an anger in me alright. He brought shame on us, he did. It was only when Miss Harriet came on the scene that I saw my chance.'

'Harriet Wilberforce, Camilla's aunt.'

'She was a lady, you see, she was above these things and she seemed to get it. I loved that woman, she took me in and gave me work and slowly I started to get back some things that I'd been robbed of. My self-respect, my place. I met Snowy, here at Brompton House. We clicked because he had his own troubles, his own anger, if you know what I mean. She looked after us both, Miss Wilberforce did, even when other folk didn't want to know us.'

'Yes. Thank you both for being so candid. That's very helpful.'

Butterfield swivelled slowly, this way and that, until his gaze fell on Jacob, 'The child, Marcia and Arthur's child. He grew up and became the smiling sailor in that little framed picture, didn't he?'

Jacob smiled and nodded, 'He did that.'

'Tell us what he was like, Jacob, back in those days.'

Jacob folded his arms and leaned back to tell his story, 'Well now, I was only eighteen when I first set eyes on him, on my first ship in the merchant navy. So he was a good bit older, in his early thirties, and he knew the ropes. I suppose you could say he took me under his wing. That's the way he was, everybody liked him, he could make you smile, and he knew stuff. He could talk about things he'd seen, things he'd discovered on his travels. Barney was a bit of a collector and he'd show me things he'd picked up from different places; not daft, silly stuff or souvenirs…everything like the other guys bought, no, these were special, prints and paintings and old maps.

He taught me how to look at things properly; I mean everything from the smallest bird or fish to the clouds in the sky. I hung onto every word, that's how it was with us. Sometimes, he would tell me little things about his childhood but not much, he preferred to talk about the present not the past. I remember he said that he reckoned his real parents came from this part of the world, and he mentioned a few places around here.'

'How do you think he knew this?'

'I haven't a clue, someone must have told him, somewhere along the line, I suppose.'

Marcia waved her hand in the air and quickly withdrew it when all heads turned to her, 'I can't be certain, of course, but I imagine it may well have been Henry Cattermole who informed him of his family roots. That would have been typical of him, to keep a link with the child, my child, however tenuous that link was over the years.'

Ethel straightened up, sharply when Butterfield nodded in her direction.

'Whatever Barney Sutton knew of his roots, and regardless of how much he understood, he finished up back here in Clamford, at his allotment hut.'

Ethel looked across at Marcia who remained impassive.

'He turned up at the big house here, one day, wanting to help in the gardens with the other locals. Nobody knew him from Adam, but Snowy took him on and said he was a good grafter, good with the plants. He came, maybe, a couple of mornings a week, always cheerful. We just called him Barney. Her ladyship, Miss Harriet, she used to chat to him and then he started to come a bit more often. I'd see the two of them laughing and joking under the sycamore and sometimes he even got to go inside the Hall. He seemed nice and friendly enough, so we made little of it. When he got his allotment, he came far less, spent most of his time down there in his little wooden hut. Miss Wilberforce, Harriet, she used to visit him, more and more. That got Snowy and me curious. You know how it is in these parts, folk like to know about others, don't they? One day, Snowy just come out with it and asked her ladyship about Barney. Nothing too much, you understand, we're not nosey like that, just curious. That's when she let slip his name: Sutton. Funny that we didn't know it until then. Snowy said he knew summat was up as soon as the name slipped from her tongue, she went pale and got flustered. That wasn't like her at all.'

'Snowy told you that Barney's name was Sutton.'

'Straight away. I remember. We had a good drink at home to settle ourselves. Snowy reckoned as long as he stayed away at the allotment and kept himself to himself down there, no real harm could come of it, but I always knew, deep down, that it would spell trouble, I just felt it in my blood.

'Trouble?'

'You know what I mean. It would bring it all back to our door, everything we'd put behind us, it would spoil it all for us, bring back all the shame and gossip, just when we'd built a nice little life for ourselves.'

'So, what did you do…when you found out Barney Sutton was who he was and back in the area?'

'Nothing. We kept a lid on it, which wasn't easy. Snowy said he saw little Barney, anyway. We hoped it would stay that way, and it did.'

'You didn't wish to meet…your half-brother?'

Ethel looked daggers at Butterfield, 'No brother of mine.'

'You wished him harm, though.'

'No, well, not back then, as long as he kept away. Then, after Miss Harriet passed on, God rest her soul, we heard that he'd died as well. So, he was out of the picture. Gone. The last trace of that bugger of a father of mine.'

'That's what you hoped, but it didn't turn out that way did it, Ethel? It wasn't the last trace, as you put it, was it? The last trace turned up in the garden shed, here at Brompton Hall, in the shape of a tiny photograph.'

'Aye, the damned photograph…sorry Miss Bennett.'

Another swivel from Butterfield and the finger pointed, once more, towards Jacob, 'You knew all along who the sailor was, why didn't you say anything? What was the big secret?'

'You don't have to ask me that, really, do you Mr Butterfield?'

'I'll let that pass.'

'Toconom.'

'I beg your pardon?'

'Nothing, you carry on Mr Butterfield.'

'So, who else saw the photograph of Barney the sailor man?'

Trevor piped up, 'I saw it when Jacob had finished working on the frame. It was a funny thing, I thought I recognised the friendly smile, that look on his face, know what I mean?'

Camilla was nodding furiously, 'Me too. It was a little unsettling to tell the truth.'

Smiling now, Butterfield turned back to Ethel, 'It was more than a little unsettling for you, wasn't it?'

Ethel was silent for almost a minute but finally straightened, gave a little cough and began, 'I was scared. This Jacob was stirring things up good and proper, raking stuff up, poking around where it could only bring trouble to our door. Snowy said to let it lie, and we had a couple of drinks and then a few more and then we argued and had a right old fight and he got himself drunk, which is always his way when he's rattled. He was mortal drunk that night and I lay there, sobbing, in our bed, listening to him snoring away like nothing was amiss. I went downstairs and drank some vodka we had left over in the sideboard and I put my clothes on over my nightdress and I ran out into the night, on my own, in the middle of the night, or it might have been the wee early hours, I can't remember. All I know is that I had to get rid of that bloody photograph and anything else to do with Barney Sutton.'

'You took matches?'

'We always have matches lying about, Snowy liked his pipe at home.'

'You went straight to Brompton Hall?'

'Yes, I can't remember getting there, but it didn't seem to take very long in the night. The moon was out, I could see the scarecrow.'

'Arthur.'

'Arthur, aye. I got hold of the bloody thing and flung it towards the shed. I meant no harm to anyone, I just wanted the lot to disappear. It went up quick, like. As soon as the flames shot up, I panicked. The heat and the flames made it real, you see. I ran towards it and I could see the scarecrow's head melting and I grabbed it and burned my arm. The heat was too much, it was out of control, so I legged it back home, running and crying.'

'And the next morning, when you'd sobered up? What then Ethel?'

'Well, Snowy was like a bear with a sore head and I never stopped crying.'

'You were in pain, your hands and arms.'

'No, it wasn't just the burns, it was the shame of what I'd done. Snowy went off it and he was stomping about, he didn't want to go to work at Brompton, so he just hung around the house, moping and fretting. Then he seemed to settle himself down a bit. In the end, he said he was thinking of admitting to it all and handing himself over, and we fought and argued all over again. It was terrible, knowing folks would guess who the culprits were, blaming kids and pointing fingers at each other and such. It couldn't go on. Snowy got as angry as I've seen him and that's saying summat, but he couldn't stop me, I had to confess. You know what happened next, Mister Butterfield. I gave my statement, and I thought that would be that. I was willing to take my punishment and, to be honest, I felt a bit of relief that, somehow, it was all out in the open. But Snowy, he was mad as hell. He blamed Jacob, you see, thought if he hadn't showed up then none of this would have happened. Stupid, eh? Honest to God, I didn't think he'd do anything so bad as that. I don't think I'll ever get over this. My Snowy shooting somebody and taking his own life, just like that. Something must have just snapped in his brain. I'm so sorry, I just can't believe what's happened, I can't.'

She sobbed into Camilla's arms, and the room fell silent.

CHAPTER THIRTY-FOUR

Joey had never looked so good. Ted reached out his hand to feel the gentle convex curve of the old horse's crest, warm and hard beneath his palm. Perhaps, he thought, the most startling change was in the creature's eyes, alert, watchful, sparkling in the fresh morning air enveloping the farmyard.

'He's ready to be ridden again, aren't you, boy?'

Jacob's mouth relaxed into a grin that Ted had not seen before.

'Do you really think so, Jacob? Or does he need a couple more weeks of good grazing, he's getting on a bit, after all?'

'Nah, Ted, he's ready. He always tells me when he's ready.'

Jacob led Joey in a circle around the yard, methodical and rhythmic, Joey's broad head nodding slowly in his leather muzzle as Ted watched on, hands deep in pockets.

Ted had not allowed himself to think too much about this moment and now that it had arrived, he felt his throat tighten, his shoulders stiffen. These past few weeks, he knew his body felt somehow lighter because of this man, 'Where will you ride him? You're welcome to use our field, you know that.'

'I know and I'm grateful, truly I am. But, it's time we were on our way.'

'But there's plenty needs doing around here. What about Brompton Hall, they'll miss you over there?'

'They'll be fine. Trevor and Fred have everything in hand.'

'But, where will you go?'

'First, I'm going to pay a visit to Miss Bennett to tell her everything I remember about her son Barney. I want to do that 'cos she deserves to know what a fine man he was.'

'Aye, then what?'

'We'll see. Anyway, it won't be for a few days, I expect.'

Ted walked without seeing, behind Jacob and Joey, out into the meadow behind the cow barn, feeling the rush of blood in his ears, imagining horse and rider trotting slowly along trails he would never see or know. God help me, what will I do when they've gone?

From the kitchen window, Doris watched their procession, biting down on the tip of her tongue. The boys, Stuart and Phil had finally taken on the responsibility of running the farm and in the evenings they were sometimes too tired to talk much or even walk down to the Fox and Grape. There was little conversation in the house anymore, Ted was retreating further and further into his own world and she was now outside of the circle. She missed the way she used to catch him out with his little silver hip flask of brandy. This man Jacob had been a breath of fresh air, she was forced now into this realisation, Ted had come alive again, just enough to give her hope…

Her hands were still deep in a soapy washing-up bowl when the low sound of a car engine approached and forced her to look away towards the main farm gates where a plain black saloon turned in from the main village road. She didn't recognise it.

Doris was still drying her hands on a small towel as she stepped out into the yard, squinting in the sun, to greet the unexpected visitor. When the driver finally stepped out of his car, he was not someone she was expecting, 'Mister Butterfield, what brings you here? I thought all that nasty business was over and done with.'

She folded her arms; the towel tucked into her apron pocket.

'Good afternoon, Mrs Smailes. Just a quick visit, nothing to worry about, I'm just tying up a few loose ends, that's all. My word, but it's a fine day isn't it?'

'It is that, lad. You'd best come inside, I'll put the kettle on.'

'No need thanks, I think I spotted your husband just now, in the field over there.'

'You spotted right, he's with Jacob, trotting the horse, shall I call them over?'

'It's ok, thanks, I'll stretch my legs, the walk will do me good. I won't keep him long.'

The horse, ears pricked and eyes wide and alert, seemed to sense Butterfield's presence before Ted and Jacob were aware of his shadow on the warm grass at their feet.

'He looks happy enough, doesn't he?'

'Mister Butterfield, this is a surprise, what can we do for you?'

'Please, no need for formalities any more, just call me Phil. I wanted to have a few words with you, Jacob, no offence Ted, if that's alright.'

Jacob flicked the rope one more time and called Joey to a slow trot and, finally, to a complete stop, 'No problem. Tell you what, Ted, if it's ok with you, why don't you take Joey over to the stable for his feed, I'll come over shortly and check him over.'

Ted gave a nod and took hold of the rope, smiling and whispering gently in the old horse's ear, when they were out of earshot, Jacob turned to Phil Butterfield, 'The Smailes family has been good to me and Joey, and I'll tell you something else, Ted hasn't lost his way with horses, I suppose it never leaves you really, he's a good man.'

'He's going to miss you, Jacob, when you go.'

'How do you know I'm goin' anywhere?'

'Call it a sixth sense. Some folks call it a copper's nose.'

'I suppose that never leaves you, either.'

'Well, you might be right there.'

Butterfield slapped his palms across the front of his sports jacket, a little too eagerly, and began to search for something in his jacket pockets.

'I reckon it's in your trouser pocket, Phil.'

'What?'

'The piece of paper you're looking for, the one with the word written on it.'

'How did you know I was…'

'Call it a sixth sense.'

'Touché.'

Jacob laughed out loud and placed a large hand on Butterfield's shoulder, 'I've been waiting for you to ask me about the word. All the way through this business I've been waiting and wondering when you were going to ask me about Toconom, so go on then, ask me.'

Butterfield examined his shoes for a second or two, then slowly withdrew the piece of paper from his trouser pocket, 'Toconom. I know it's Monocot spelt backwards and Monocot is the name of the orchid family. Right? But, why that word? Why not daffodil or geranium?'

Jacob shoved his hands deep into his pockets, his gleeful eyes shining into Butterfield's, taking in everything he saw in the policeman's weary but wise old face, direct, earthy and curious.

'It's all about beauty, my friend. Barney Sutton had a beautiful soul, and it shone through him, all the time, even when him and me were cooped up on a ship among hundreds of sweaty men surrounded by nothing but the ocean, he could see beauty in everything. He loved orchids, and he loved having fun. It was as if he wanted everyone else to see what he could see. I was young and impressionable and vulnerable and he took me under his wing, like. He taught me how to look at things, how to have fun with nowt in your pocket. Like it was a language you have to learn. He wrote backwards sometimes, or upside down, back to front; taught himself to do stuff like that 'cos it was fun, like a special code you have to break before you could see the beauty. Orchids were his favourites. He showed me the orchid fields in Singapore, I remember that. Just me and him. It was beauty and fun, simple as that. He told me, once, when he was a nipper, he taught himself these things to help him kill the sadness in his world where he grew up, in a home for kids.'

'Kill the sadness.'

'That's what he said, Mr Butterfield, and I knew that's what I had to do. I had to be like him, know what I mean?'

'Yes, I think I do. So now tell me, has it worked? Has it killed the sadness?'

Jacob folded his arms, sensing something different behind the creased old eyes that were almost pleading for answers, noticing the grey in his hair and sideburns; he hadn't shaved properly this morning.

'Well now, Mister Butterfield, or can I call you Phil? How can I best explain? There are things we all regret, stuff we wish we said different or done a different way and I am no different to everybody else. But the one thing I will never regret is listening hard to Barney Sutton and taking it all in as best as I could. So I have to say yes, he took away my sadness, but you are asking me 'cos there's stuff on your mind. I'm right, aren't I?'

'You are a very perceptive man, Jacob.'

'Takes one to know one, Phil.'

Butterfield stiffened, it had been a long time since he questioned anyone quite like this man, he could taste bile at the back of his throat as he coughed. Today, standing in this warm field, he didn't like too much the man he'd become. He preferred the old crafty copper he used to be, not this guy who was about to retire only to discover what he'd been missing through all these years, 'Do you think Ethel burned the shed down out of anger, shame, a moment of madness or what? And did Snowy shoot himself out of rage or despair? What do you think, eh? Are they to be condemned or pitied? I've been asking myself these questions, you see. That's what's on my mind, Jacob. What pushed them over the edge?'

'There is no edge. Not really. There's just life, our own lives, we create edges in our heads, in our dreams but they're not real. I reckon that's what Barney would have said, or summat like it.'

'Maybe he was right.'

'He was right.'

Philip Butterfield blinked hard. Everything around the two of them seemed to disappear for a second or two. This was ever so slightly ridiculous; an ordinary conversation in many ways, but if he'd learnt anything during his police career, it was surely this:

there was always something special and important in the smallest of moments. Jacob turned on his heels and began to walk back towards the stable barn where Ted was feeding Joey and brushing him down. Butterfield was at Jacob's side, and as their shadows fell in front of them on the dry ground, reality returned.

'Phil, what are you doing the rest of the day?'

'Nothing planned, a few reports to write up but they can wait, why?'

'I was thinking of going over to see Marcia Bennett at the care home. I won't take Joey, not there, but if you could take me in your car, I'd be much obliged, like.'

'No problem.'

CHAPTER THIRTY-FIVE

She sat in her armchair holding the little framed photograph in her lap, head erect, alert, listening to Jacob with such intensity it almost frightened her. At last, she breathed out gently and slowly, when he finished speaking. Butterfield sat quietly in the corner of her room, clutching a porcelain cup half filled with tea gone cold.

When Marcia spoke, her calm assurance was a surprise to both men, 'Thank you. I used to dream of a moment like this. Thank you, you have brought him to life for me. It's quite astonishing the fantasies one can weave together. Barney was my son, yet he was just a dream; I pictured him in different ways for so many years do you see? The photograph was of great comfort, of course, but, today, you have put some flesh on the bones of someone who has been more like a ghost to me than my own flesh and blood.'

'I'm not one for fancy language, Miss Bennett, but let me just say this, he's been my inspiration, all my life. That's the truth, honest.'

'You have a very good way with words, Jacob, but I'm sure you know as much, really.'

'Say what you mean and mean what you say. It's what I try to do, that's all.'

'Quite right.'

And with this, she eased herself out of her chair to place Barney's photograph next to the old priest, Rev Henry Cattermole. In that moment, Butterfield knew he must speak up or lose this opportunity forever. But the words still wouldn't come.

'Philip, you're silent.'

Marcia wasn't even looking at him when she spoke, she was brushing her hands over the pleats of her skirt and plucking away at the sleeves of her cardigan; yet no one, not even the darkest of criminals, had ever caught him off guard so effectively as this serene and unassuming lady. She turned her face gently upward, her kind eyes inviting him to smile and respond, and something which had buried itself deep in his stomach until it hardened to a rock, overheated and melted away.

'Sorry, Marcia, I was just listening to everything Jacob was saying, that's all.'

'And why is that? I thought your work in Clamford was done, case closed.'

'Yes, yes, it is, but I …'

'Come now, you and I have known each other a long time, so why don't you explain what's on your mind…please.'

'Well, I er…'

'Why are you so interested in hearing about my long-lost son, Barney? I can see he meant a great deal to Jacob here, and to those who met him when he was alive, but you…?'

Butterfield straightened in his chair, fists like two large cricket balls resting on his knees, 'Because Barney was my brother, and I never met him, never wanted to, and I am ashamed.'

'What you mean is, Philip, is that Barney was your half-brother, because you are Arthur Sutton's son.'

She knew all along.

Butterfield could hardly make his body move. Slowly, his hand went to his dry mouth, and the words came, 'Arthur Sutton was a lady's man, immoral rather than downright evil, charming but slippery. He was the man who nearly broke up our family when he took up with my mother. Dad forgave her, but there was always a shadow hanging over everything in our house and the shadow was me. Don't get me wrong, my father was a good man, and he raised me up to be a good man, but there was always a shadow. I wasn't his, I was made by Arthur Sutton. You can't hide something like that, eventually, it'll come out and bite you; on your records, your blood group, your medical history, stuff like that, could be anything, but it'll always be there. Evidence. My world. My folks broke it to me when I was about eight or nine when I had to go into hospital to have my tonsils out and there were problems, I haemorrhaged and needed a blood transfusion or something. They told me his name was Arthur but nothing more. All I knew was he'd scarpered off, left the area and no one really knew where the hell he was. They said to forget him. So I did. At least, I tried my best to. We got through it. Like I say, I was brought up kindly and well, my parents were good to me and I had to be a good lad, make them proud, do the right things. Always. I set my mind to do right by them. I became a copper. Coppers are nosey by nature and instinct and, well…'

'When did you know for sure, that Arthur Sutton was your real father?'

'I was in denial about it, I suppose, for a long time, but it was during the investigation, and when I saw the photograph and…well, you know what happened.'

Jacob drew breath and leaned forward, 'Why are you ashamed, Phil? You've nothing to be ashamed about as far as I can see.'

They sat in silence in Marcia's bedroom until the sound of a trolley passed down the corridor, breaking the ice.

'Do you know how shame really feels when it cuts into you? Because I know how Ethel Elstop felt when she set alight to the shed and I know how desperate Snowy must have felt. Do you think that's barmy, over the top? That's what the copper in me says but let me tell you…the anger, frustration builds up and you just want revenge, you can taste it. I hate the feeling. I never want to feel it again. Wasted lives, misery, regret, injury and death because one man, years ago, couldn't keep his manhood in his trousers. I wouldn't be here, right now, living and breathing, if it wasn't for that bastard; makes me feel shame. It does. Cos I know I could easily be driven to do what Ethel did, that sort of hurt and shame stays with you and burns away, angry, waiting to come out.'

Marcia nodded, half smiling as the words spilled out of him, but she said nothing, letting his last sentence settle, like a cloud of dust floating down upon an old carpet. Then she clicked her tongue and spoke crisply.

'Yet, neither you nor my son inherited your father's undoubted faults. Surely, that is what matters here. I am pleased you came today. You too, Jacob.'

'TOCONOM.'

CHAPTER THIRTY-SIX

Jacob narrowed his eyes, silent, upright in the passenger seat. Next to him, Philip Butterfield's heart was beating faster behind the wheel as he steered the car through the Smailes's farm gates towards the ambulance.

'What the hell's happened now?' was all he could manage, his eyes scanning the scene, tension constricting his throat.

Stu Smailes stood with his arms at his sides as his brother Phil, stooped and sullen, listened intently to a young paramedic.

Over by the stable block, the old horse Joey whinnied and watched on, his head drooping slightly but his ears pricked, alert.

Butterfield followed Jacob, slow-footed, towards the ambulance; Doris was in the back, hunched over the still, lifeless body of her husband.

Stuart was the first to break ranks, turning towards Butterfield and Jacob with a tiny wave of the arm, 'He's gone, Jacob, there's nowt more they can do for him. All over in seconds.'

'How? What happened?'

'Heart attack.'

Jacob wrapped an arm around Stuart's shoulder and walked a few yards with him, nodding sympathetically as they trod a slow circle around the yard; then he left him alone and turned towards the stable and stayed there with Joey, gently whispering into the old piebald's ear.

Doris was helped down from the ambulance, and Butterfield was by her side in a moment, 'I'm so sorry Doris, this is a terrible shock. Why don't we get you inside? I'll put the kettle on while the lads do what they have to do, come on.'

She threaded her arm through the crook of his, 'You won't find us very presentable today, I'm afraid.'

The kitchen was warm from the steady sun, the bananas in the fruit bowl had ripened and needed eating up, and some lunch time pots were waiting to be washed and cleared away.

'It all happened so quick d'you see? I was watching him over by the stable, brushing down the horse, smiling away he was, so I just boiled the kettle and I filled his favourite mug and took it over for him. But, when I got there, he'd already keeled over, collapsed on the ground by the horse's hooves, still with the brush in his hand. His eyes were half closed, so I got down on my knees and I took away the brush and held his hand. He was saying something, or trying to speak I should say.'

'What was he trying to say, do you think?'

'Dunno, it was rubbish really, but at least he was smiling while he was trying to talk. I wanted to get up to call the ambulance straight away, but he gripped my hand tighter. Lucky that Stuart was close by, I shouted to him to call them out. Ted made me smile then, what he was saying I mean, and so I thought he was going to be alright…'

'He was smiling, that's a good thing to remember, Doris.'

'I suppose so. He was rambling away. He said we must get everything tidied up in case the King came by again. I said to him to rest, but he carried on. He said he thought the King seems to like the place and how he was ever such a nice chap. I just let him ramble on and we waited for the medics to come. But, then he just closed his eyes and went to sleep. Just like that.'

'I'm so sorry.'

'Aye. Thank you. It hasn't sunk in yet. Shock and that. But, I tell you what Mr Butterfield…'

'Phil.'

'Aye. Phil, his last days were happy ones because of that man out there with the old horse. Jacob. I should thank him for what he did. You see, I knew my Ted wasn't right, I knew it for over a year. This way, folk will remember Ted the way he was, how he used to be. Ted liked Jacob, said he cheered him up, made him feel right with the world. He's a good man and I'll be forever grateful that he was here these past weeks. If he wants to stay in the old cottage, he'll be welcome.'

Outside in the yard, Jacob quietly walked Joey out away from the ambulance towards the farm gates; the old horse almost broke into a trot, tossing his head, his pace steady and sure as if he was young again.

'Easy boy, easy.'

Soon, they had reached the village square and the little school, then Millers shop and the Fox and Grape. The pavements were quiet as they passed, not a soul in the church grounds of St Barnabas's.

He felt the soft touch of the horse's muzzle on his fingers and knew that Joey would not wander off while he entered the tiny cottage. It was clean and tidy. He was gone for only a minute before he emerged with the old travel bag and saddle. Soon, they arrived at the bridge where Joey's hooves clattered on the hard surface as they crossed the slow river beneath. At the statue of the naked Harriet Wilberforce, they paused for a second or two. When a momentary rush of sad regret arrived and fled quickly, they proceeded up the hill, away from Clamford. Twenty yards away, the sun bounced off the bonnet of a gleaming Land Rover; inside, someone was speaking into a phone.

Jacob stopped abruptly when something, over on a small ridge, caught his eye.; he noticed the other man before his horse did.

He was sitting by a fence, deep in concentration but from such a distance there was no way of knowing whether he was writing, sketching or painting a view of the Vale. Drawing nearer, Jacob rubbed his eyes with the heels of his hands as the man glanced up from his work and put on a pair of dark spectacles. Smiling, his face was instantly recognisable.

Once astride his old horse again, Jacob called over, 'Your Majesty, TOCONOM.'

ABOUT THE AUTHOR

David Hay lives in Long Newton, a village between Stockton on Tees and Darlington, with his wife, Pat.

He is the author of six novels:

The Tower House
A Smile to Tempt a Lover
The Wisdom of the Wise
A Suit of Black
Mr. Lambert's Dream
A Word to the Wise

The Wisdom of the Wise won the Page Turner Award for best e-book.
A Word to the Wise is the sequel.

Printed in Great Britain
by Amazon